wtf

**More jaw-dropping reads
from Simon Pulse**

exit here.
Jason Myers

fml
Shaun David Hutchinson

Break
Hannah Moskowitz

Rush
Jeremy Iversen

Crash
Lisa McMann

wtf

Peter Lerangis

Simon Pulse

New York   London   Toronto   Sydney   New Delhi

SIMON PULSE
An imprint of Simon & Schuster Children's Publishing Division
1230 Avenue of the Americas, New York, NY 10020
This Simon Pulse edition June 2013
Copyright © 2009 by Peter Lerangis
All rights reserved, including the right of reproduction in whole or in part in any form.
SIMON PULSE and colophon are registered trademarks of Simon & Schuster, Inc.
For information about special discounts for bulk purchases, please contact Simon & Schuster Special Sales at 1-866-506-1949 or business@simonandschuster.com.
The Simon & Schuster Speakers Bureau can bring authors to your live event. For more information or to book an event contact the Simon & Schuster Speakers Bureau at 1-866-248-3049 or visit our website at www.simonspeakers.com.
Designed by Mike Rosamilia
The text of this book was set in Warnock Pro.
Manufactured in the United States of America
2 4 6 8 10 9 7 5 3 1
Library of Congress Control Number 2005937182
ISBN 978-1-4424-9369-8 (hc)
ISBN 978-1-4424-9368-1 (trade pbk)
ISBN 978-1-4169-1360-3 (5x7 pbk)
ISBN 978-1-4391-6062-6 (eBook)

With thanks to:
Bethany Buck, for getting the ball rolling;
Anica Rissi, for keeping it out of the gutter; and
Michael del Rosario, for resetting the pins

PART ONE
IT BEGINS

1

JIMMY
October 17, 9:07 P.M.

The eyes were beautiful.

They were mad huge, anime-hero huge, staring out of the darkness.

Something brushed his cheek too, rhythmically. Like kisses.

Jimmy smiled.

Kisses happened all the time to guys like Cam, who expected them. Never to Jimmy.

So he would always remember that moment, how weirdly tender and exciting it was on that deserted road on that rainy October evening, before he blinked and realized his world had gone to shit.

2

9:08 P.M.

It wasn't the taste of blood that brought him to reality. Or the rain pelting his face through the jagged shark-jaw where the windshield had been. Or the car engine, screaming like a vacuum cleaner on steroids. Or the glass in his teeth.

It was the sight of Cam's feet.

They were thick, forceful feet, Sasquatch feet whose size you knew because Cam bragged about it all the time (14EE), feet that seemed to be their own form of animal life. But right now, in a pool of dim light just below the passenger seat, they looked weightless and demure, curved like a ballerina's. One flip-flop had fallen off, but both legs were moving listlessly with the rhythm of the black mass that lay across the top half of Cam's body—the mass that was attached to the eyes that were staring up at Jimmy.

"Shit!"

Jimmy lurched away. The animal was twitching, smacking its nose against his right arm now, flinging something foamy and warm all over the car. It was half in and half out, its hindquarters resting on the frame of the busted windshield, its haunches reaching out over the hood. The broken remains of a mounted handheld GPS device hung from the dash like an incompletely yanked tooth.

For a moment he imagined he was home, head down on his desk, his mom nudging him awake with a cup of hot cocoa. It was Friday night. He was always home on Friday night. But this was real, and he remembered now—the deer springing out of the darkness, running across the road, legs pumping, neck strained. . . .

"CAAAAAM! BYRON!"

His voice sounded dull, muffled by the rain's ratatat-ting on the roof. No one answered. Not Byron in the back-seat.

Not Cam.

Cam.

Was he alive? He wasn't crying out. Wasn't saying a thing.

Jimmy fumbled for the door handle. His fingers were

cold and numb. With each movement the engine screamed, and he realized his right foot was stuck against the accelerator, trapped between it and a collapsed dashboard. He tried to pull it out and squeeze the door handle, but both were stuck. He gave up on his foot and looked for the lock.

There.

The door fell open with a metallic *grrrrrock.* Jimmy hung on to the armrest, swinging out with the door, as a red pickup sped by. It swerved to avoid him, and Jimmy tried to shout for help. His foot still stuck, he spilled out headfirst, twisting so his shoulders hit the pavement. As his teeth snapped shut, blood oozed over his bottom lip. He spat tiny glass particles.

The pickup was racing away, past a distant streetlight, which cast everything in a dim, smoky glow. From the car's windshield, the deer's hind legs kicked desperately in silhouette, like the arms of a skinny cheerleader pumping a victory gesture.

As Jimmy yanked his own leg, not caring if the fucking thing came off at the ankle, he felt the rain washing away the blood. Through the downpour he could see the long, furry face on the seat—nodding, nodding, as if in sympathy. *That's it, pal. Go. Go. Go.*

His ankle pulled loose, and he tumbled backward

onto the road, legs arcing over his head. As he lay still, catching his breath, he heard someone laugh, a desperate, high-pitched sound piercing the rain's din.

It took a moment before he realized it was his own voice.

3

9:09 P.M.

"Jesus, it's still alive!"

Byron's voice. From the backseat.

Byron was okay.

Jimmy jumped up from the road. He struggled to keep upright, his leg numb. He spat his mouth clean as he made his way around the car. Through the side window he could see Byron's silhouette, peering over the front seat. Jimmy looked through the driver's side window. The deer's back was enormous, matted with blood and flecks of windshield. Under it he could make out only the right side of Cam's body from the shoulder down, but not his face.

Cam was completely smothered.

"Oh God, Jimmy, what did you do?" Byron said.

"I—I don't know. . . . It just, like, *appeared*!" Jimmy

had to grip the side of the car to keep from falling, or flying away, or completely disintegrating. He blinked, trying desperately to find the right angle, hoping to see a sign that Cam was alive. "Push it, Byron—push it off!"

"It's a monster—how the fuck am I supposed to push it? *Shit, Jimmy, how could you have not seen it?*"

"*I did!*" Jimmy screamed. "I braked. I tried to get out of the way—"

"Dickwad! You tried to outmaneuver a *deer*? You don't *brake*! That makes the grill drop lower—lifts the animal right up into the car, like a fucking spoon! You just *drive*. That way you smack it right back into the woods."

"*If you know so much, why weren't you driving?*"

"With what license?"

"*I don't have one either!*"

"You told me you did!"

"I never told you that! I just said I knew how to drive. I never took the test—"

"Oh, great—the only person in Manhattan our age who knows how to drive, *and you don't bother to get a license.*" Byron leaned closer, suddenly looking concerned. "Jesus Christ, what happened to your mouth?"

"It's what I get for applying lipstick without a mirror—"

"Awwww, *shit!*" Byron was looking at something in his hand. "My BlackBerry's totaled."

"How can you think about your BlackBerry while Cam is under the deer?"

Byron looked up with a start, then immediately leaped out of the car. "Oh fuck, Cam. Is he dead?"

"'*Oh fuck, Cam*'? You just noticed him? You're yelling at me, and you just thought of Cam?" Jimmy's hands trembled as he pulled his cell phone out of his pocket. "I'm calling 911."

"No, don't!" Byron said, snatching the phone from Jimmy's hand.

"Are you crazy?" Jimmy said. "What's wrong with you?"

"We're in East Dogshit and the GPS is busted—do you even know what road we're on? What are you going to tell the cops? *Um, there's this tree? And, like, a ditch? And a road?* And then what, we wait? We don't have time, Jimmy!"

"But—"

"Think it through, Einstein. What's your story? One, you wrecked a car that's not yours. Two, you don't have a license. Three, you killed a deer. And four, look at Cam. You planning to go to Princeton and room with Rhodes scholars? How about a guy with three teeth who can't wait for you to bend over? Because if we don't stop talking, dude, you're facing murder charges."

"He's not dead, Byron—"

"Just put the fucking phone away and let's get Bambi off Cam." Byron threw Jimmy the phone and raced to the back of the car. "Throw me the keys. I'll get a rope out of the trunk. When I give you back the keys, get in the car."

Jimmy reached into the car, tossing the phone onto the dashboard. Quickly removing the keys from the steering column, he threw them to Byron. He eyed the driver's seat. The deer was still moving, still trying to get away. *No way* was he going back in there.

But he couldn't abandon Cam.

If only he could think straight. His brain was useless. In that moment, he was picturing a cloud of small, hungry ticks hovering over the front seat. He tried to shake it off, but it was like some weird psychological hijacking brought on by his mother's lifelong vigil over the mortal threat posed by proximity to deer, which turned every suburban outing into a preparation for war.

"What are you fucking worried about, Lyme's disease?" Byron shouted. "Get in there!"

Jimmy cringed. "It's *Lyme*," he muttered, grabbing the door handle. "Not *Lyme's*."

"What?" Byron shouted.

"Nothing. What am I supposed to do—in the car?"

"What the fuck do you think you're supposed to do?"

As if in response, the deer gave a sudden shudder. Jimmy jumped back, stifling a scream. "I—I'm not sure . . ."

"When I give the word, put it in reverse, Jimmy. And gun it."

Byron yanked open the trunk and threw the keys to Jimmy, who kept a wary eye on the deer as he opened the door. It was motionless now, its snout resting just below the gear shift.

As Jimmy climbed inside, the car rocked with Byron's efforts to shove stuff under the rear tires for traction.

Breathe in. Breathe out.

Jimmy tried to stop himself from hyperventilating. He eyed Cam's feet, blinking back tears. He had never liked Cam, or any of the smart-ass jocks who treated the Speech Team kids like they were some kind of lower life-form. Since freshman year he had devoted a lot of time conjuring horrible fates for most of them, fates not unlike this.

In . . . Out . . .

Jimmy hadn't wanted to go on this drive. It was Byron who'd pushed the idea. *Cam* wants us to go, *Cam* says suburban parties are the best ever, *Cam* says Westchester chicks are hot for NYC guys. *Cam* wants to be friends. It would be stupid to miss a chance at détente between the worlds of sports and geekdom.

In . . .

Until this time, Jimmy couldn't imagine that Byron would be friends with a guy like Cam. Byron the potty-mouthed genius, Cam the football guy. Was this some kind of crush? Was *that* the reason for—

"Wake up, douche bag!" Byron shouted. "Now! *Go!*"

With his foot on the brake, Jimmy threw the car in reverse. The accelerator was touching the bottom of the caved-in dashboard. Carefully, he wedged his foot in and floored it.

The engine roared to life, the tires gripping the debris. As the car lurched backward, the deer's head rose slowly off the seat with the force of the rope. Something warm spattered against the side of Jimmy's face.

"AAAGHH!" he screamed, yanking his foot away from the accelerator.

"*WHAT?*" Byron cried, running around the side of the car. "Why'd you stop? We almost had it!"

"It puked on me!"

Byron shone a flashlight into the front seat. "It's not puke. It's blood."

"Oh, great . . ." Jimmy's stomach flipped. *This couldn't be happening!*

"Here. This'll protect you." Byron was throwing something over the animal's head—a rag, a blanket, it was impossible to see. "Don't think about it, Jimmy. Just step on it! And put on your seat belt."

Jimmy felt a lightness in his head. His eyes were crossing. *Focus.*

He buckled his belt and put the car in reverse again, slipping his foot under the wreckage of the dashboard. As he floored it, the car began to move, the engine roaring. The animal's hulk rose up beside him, away from him—scraping across the bottom of the windshield, slowly receding out of the car and onto the hood.

The blanket fell off the deer's head, as the carcass finally slipped off, the car jerked backward.

SMMMMACK!

Jimmy's head whipped against the headrest. He bounced back, his chest catching the seat belt and knocking the wind out of him.

"Are you okay?" Byron cried.

"Fah—fah—" Everything was white. Jimmy struggled to breathe, his eyes slowly focusing on the image in the rearview mirror, the twisted metal of a guardrail reflecting against the taillights.

Byron was leaning in the open passenger window, training a flashlight on the dim silhouette of Cam's lifeless body, now freed from the deer. "This does not look good. . . ." he said.

"Is his chest moving?"

"I don't know! I don't think so, but I can't—" In the distance a muffled siren burst through the rain's din. Byron drew back, shutting the flashlight. "Shit! Did you call them?"

"No!" Jimmy said.

"Then how do they know?"

Jimmy thought about the red pickup. "Someone drove past us, just after the accident. Maybe they called."

"Someone saw us?"

"This is a New York suburb. Occasionally people drive on the roads."

"Oh, God. Oh, God. Oh, God. Oh, shit. Oh, God." Byron was backing away from the car, disappearing into the darkness.

"I'm the one who's supposed to be freaking out, not you!" Jimmy leaned toward Cam's inert body, his hands

shaking. The cold rain, evaporating against his body, rose up in smoky wisps. *Don't be dead don't be dead please please please please don't be dead.*

"C-C-Cam?" Jimmy slapped Cam's cheek and shook his massive shoulders, but Cam was limp and unresponsive. His body began to slip on the rain-slicked seat, falling toward the driver's side. Jimmy tried to shove back, but he was helpless against the weight. Cam's head plopped heavily in Jimmy's lap.

"Aaaaghhh!" He pushed open the door, jumped out, and looked around for Byron. "I think he's . . . he's . . ."

The siren's wail was growing closer. How would he explain this? *You see, officer, in New York City no one gets a license until they're in college. But my dad taught me to drive on weekends, on Long Island. No, I don't have the registration either. The car belongs to—belonged to . . . him . . . the deceased.*

He'd have to get out of here before they came. He looked past the car. There was a gully, a hill. It was pitch-black. He could get lost in the night.

Asshole! No, the cops would figure it out. Fingerprints. Friends knew he was driving—Reina Sanchez, she had to know. She was all over Cam. She'd tell them. So it wouldn't only be manslaughter. It would also be leaving the scene of the crime. What was that? Life in prison?

Stay or go, he was screwed either way. Because of a deer. A fucking stupid deer. Without the deer, everything would have been all right.

"BYRON!" he shouted.

In the distance he heard Byron retching, with characteristic heroism.

Cam was now slumped into the driver's seat, his right shoulder touching the bottom of the steering wheel.

He used me. He convinced Byron to get me to drive so he could go to a party. And now he will never ever be accountable. Because he's . . .

Dead. He was dead. He would never move again, never talk.

And that opened up several possibilities, some of which were

Unthinkable.

An idea was taking shape cancerously fast among his battered brain cells. If you were thinking something, it wasn't unthinkable—that was Goethe, or maybe Wittgenstein, or Charlie Brown. The idea danced between the synapses, on the line between survival and absolute awfulness, presenting itself in a sick, Quentin Tarantino way that made perfect sense.

It was Cam's dad's car. It would be logical that Cam would be driving it.

No one will know.

He grabbed Cam's legs. They were heavy, dead weight. He pulled them across the car toward the driver's side, letting Cam's butt slide with them—across the bench seat, across the pool of animal blood and pebbled glass.

Jimmy lifted Cam into an upright position, but his body fell forward, his torso resting hard against the steering wheel.

HONNNNNNNNNNK!

The sound was ridiculously loud. Around the bend, distant headlights were making the curtain of rain glow. No time to fix this now.

Jimmy bolted for the woods.

"What are you doing?" Byron called out of the dark. He was standing now, peering into the car. "Jesus Christ! You're trying to *make it look like Cam drove*? What if he's alive? He'll tell them you were driving!"

Jimmy stopped, frantically looking around for something blunt. He stooped to pick up a rusted piece of tailpipe, maybe a foot long. It would do the trick. He knelt by the driver's door and drew it back.

"JIMMY, ARE YOU OUT OF YOUR FUCKING MIND?"

Byron's eyes were like softballs. He grabbed Jimmy's arm.

Jimmy let the tailpipe fall to the ground. He felt his brain whirling, his knees buckling. He felt Byron pulling him away.

As the cop cars squealed to a halt near the blaring car, he was moving fast but feeling nothing.

4

9:27 P.M.

"Request backup."

Voices crackled behind them as Jimmy's feet squelched into a puddle, ankle-deep. He stumbled upward, arms splayed out in front, grabbing unseen branches. The rain had turned the ground into a sodden mess that muffled their footfalls.

Mea culpa, mea culpa, mea maxima culpa. Mea maxima maxima culpa.

He turned to look back at the police. He could give himself up. He could demand to be delivered to the nearest church, where a kindly priest could condemn Jimmy to hell for what he'd done to his dead friend before politely giving Jimmy over to the electric chair.

"Will you come *on*?" Byron whispered.

Jimmy felt Byron's hand grabbing his shoulder, pulling him up over a fallen tree trunk.

They fell to the ground, peering over the top. Their panting was barely discernible above the racket of the rain falling on the leaves. "You okay?" Byron asked.

Below them, a cop car had pulled to a stop facing the Corolla, its headlights trained on it. For the first time Jimmy saw how bad the accident had been. The car was totaled—the front smashed in, the roof dented, the rear accordioned inward from the guardrail crash.

"I'm great, Byron. Never better. I figure if I don't get pneumonia or pleurisy or Lyme's disease or a heart attack from guilt or electrocuted by the state, you and I can go have an ice-cream soda!"

"You having some kind of PTSD moment, dude?" Byron muttered. He was shaking. "No offense, but after what you just did—*almost* did—I'm worried for my own life here."

Jimmy felt cramped, as if he'd swallowed some kind of slow-acting poison. "I—I didn't mean to do it."

"That's reassuring," Byron whispered.

"I don't know what came over me. It was like my brain just . . . just . . ." His voice drifted off.

Byron put a heavy, waterlogged arm tentatively on

Jimmy's shoulder. "Look. You . . . you were under pressure. Like, temporarily insane? And from what I saw in the car, hey, Cam's toast anyway."

"Is that supposed to be a *consolation*?" Jimmy said.

"No! What I mean is, even if you had hit him, I don't think it would have been murder, if that's what you're worried about."

"I can't believe you're saying this," Jimmy said. "Cam is a *person*! He was your friend."

Byron grabbed him by the collar, his lips retracted, his teeth seeming to float in the darkness. "You think I'm a cold, callous son of a bitch? If you really want to know, my stomach is razor blades right now, and if we talk about this another moment I'm going to cry. Or scream. Or throw you down the hill. So maybe let's just drop it."

They crouched near the ground, frozen in place. Jimmy felt the rain in his toes, running down his face, still washing blood and glass off his clothes, making his arms shrively like his grandfather's. It felt as if the rain were a part of him. The cops were training flashlights into the Corolla, barking orders into walkie-talkies. In moments another cop car screeched into view, followed by a tow truck and an ambulance emblazoned with the name POLK-BAUMAN HOSPITAL.

Jimmy watched the EMT workers quickly, efficiently pull Cam out of the car, lay him on a stretcher, and load him into the ambulance. As it pulled away, siren blaring, the tow truck hooked up the front of Cam's car.

The police officers, huddled in rain slickers, began searching the surrounding area. One of them stopped at the deer.

"Oh, Jesus . . . ," Byron muttered under his breath. *"Don't do that. . . . Please don't do that. . . ."*

"Did you take the rope off its legs?" Jimmy asked.

"Duh, what do you think?" Byron snapped. "I'm not stupid enough to forget *that*."

"So they'll think the deer bounced off the car?"

"Is that what you're worried about—whether the cops will find out what you did? Is that it, Jimmy? Is that what Cam's life means to you? Who's cold and callous now?"

"What are *you* worried about, Byron?" Jimmy snapped. "Why did *you* run away? Why aren't *you* down there giving them information? Why are you acting so fucking weird?"

Byron turned away without replying. Then he grabbed Jimmy by the arm.

Below them, the police officers were turning away from the deer, toward the woods.

"Shit. Come on!" Byron whispered.

As the two scrambled farther into the shelter of the trees, a searchlight beam swept over the log behind which they had just been lying.

5

10:03 P.M.

"John F. Kennedy swam five miles with a belt in his teeth, towing a wounded soldier," Byron called out, gasping for breath at the top of a weed-choked incline in the woods. "John McCain was in solitary confinement, with two broken arms, *for two and a half years.*"

"Good for John McCain!" said Jimmy, feeling around for his shoe that had been sucked into the mud. "What's the point?"

"The point is, *it's only a shoe!*" Byron said. "Walk barefoot. That's why God gave you feet. And besides, you shouldn't have worn those faggy Vans anyway! We get to this party, they're all going to think you're gay."

"And this is bad because . . . ?"

"You scare me, Jimmy."

"That's *your* problem." Jimmy was out of breath, sick of running in the rain, and not about to move another inch before finding his missing shoe. He and Byron had gotten lost in the woods several times, but to his credit, Byron had managed to keep his bearings by finding the occasional streetlight and following the contour of the road. Which did not stop him from being a pain in the butt the whole time. "Found it! Thanks, Byron, for your patience and sensitivity."

"Fuck you, okay? That wasn't *me* with the lead pipe back there, Mr. Congeniality." Byron winced. "Sorry. I didn't mean that. I'm cranky. Must be the rain."

Jimmy tried not to let the words in. Forcing his foot into the soggy shoe, he stood and followed Byron. They were approaching a distant cluster of lights, a group of houses at the top of a rise. Just past a pine grove, a house with big plate-glass windows was all lit up. Cars were parked all around, speckled with reflected light. "Remember the GPS?" Byron said excitedly. "Remember when it said, 'In point-six miles, turn right and go to the end of the road'? Look—check out that last house on the right."

Jimmy had never felt his heart beat like this, like it would pop out onto the ground if he didn't keep his shirt buttoned. "What do we tell them? They're Cam's friends."

Byron shook his head. "They're not. Trust me. He heard about the party on Facebook. Some football dude from another team. We walk in there and pretend we belong. We tell them our car ran out of gas and we had to walk. We're stupid New York City kids. We'll get them feeling good and superior—"

"Sooner or later people are going to hear about the accident," Jimmy said.

"By that time, we'll have convinced some yutz to drive us home or drop us at the train station."

A few feet from the house, Jimmy's knees locked. "I—I can't."

"What's wrong?"

"It's *all* wrong, Byron."

A scene was taking shape in his brain: *The day dawns on the Hong household. Cam's little sister is eating breakfast in the kitchen by herself as the sun rises over West End Avenue. She thinks about her brother as the coffee starts self-brewing, and she wonders if her dad has set it for one fewer cup. Someone appears in the doorway and it looks like Mrs. Hong, only she appears to be ten years older, her cheeks raw from tears, while across town Reina Sanchez weeps for the love of her life. . . .*

"Jimmy? You can't flake out on me now. What's done is done. We have to move on."

Jimmy imagined himself moving on, walking away, head facing straight upward, breathing in the rain, letting it drown him . . . reaching a precipice in the darkness and just stepping quietly over it. . . . "It's like a Martin Scorsese movie," he said quietly, "where someone makes one bad choice. Like, one stupid, cowardly, amoral choice he didn't really have to make, because if he did the right thing in the first place it would have been tough but way better in the long-term. But he can't see that so instead does the stupid thing, and it fucks up everybody?"

"What?"

"We shouldn't be here. We need to go to the police."

Byron spun him around and leaned close. "Jimmy. Jimmy, listen to me. You have to promise you will never, *ever* go to the police."

"It's wrong, Byron . . ."

"Say it," Byron insisted. "*Say it, Jimmy.* For your own sake. For the common sense to not totally screw up your life, everything you ever dreamed of—college, med school, business school, or whatever the fuck you want to do. Say, 'I promise I will never go to the police.'"

"What do *you* care? You weren't the one driving."

"Say it!" Byron's eyebrows and lashes dripped rain, but the strength of his gaze seemed to vaporize it.

Jimmy looked away. "Ipromiselwillnevergotothe-police. . . ."

"What?"

"I promise I will never go to the police!"

Byron held out his hand. "Give me your phone."

"Go to hell," Jimmy replied.

"Seriously. I want it."

"I already promised you." Jimmy fished around in his pocket. "Besides, I don't have it anymore."

"Bullshit."

"I don't, okay? I must have dropped it."

"What if someone finds it?"

"I'll cancel the account, okay?"

"That's not the point—"

"I don't care what the point is, Byron! I already feel like the only thing that keeps me from killing myself is the decision whether or not to kill you first—so will you shut the fuck up?"

Byron sighed. He put both hands on Jimmy's shoulders. "Okay. Sorry, dude. My bad. We're going to go in there. We're going to get dry. We're going to get drunk. And then we'll figure things out from there. Somehow we'll get ourselves home."

Jimmy nodded. Numbly, he followed Byron out of the woods and toward the light. The sound of the pounding rain picked up a bass line and transmuted into a loud hip-hop track.

6

10:19 P.M.

"Dude, you look like a fucking chicken. What happened?"

The guy asking the question was skinny and had an Adam's apple that resembled a trapped peach. He was exactly the kind of overgroomed, khaki-pantsed future Ivy Leaguer who seemed to gravitate to speech teams, to Jimmy's constant horror. Only this guy seemed a couple of ounces away from incoherence, his right hand wrapped around a drink in a McDonald's collector sippy cup exactly like the ones Jimmy remembered from his fourth-grade summer vacation trip to Yellowstone National Park. "We hit a deer," Jimmy said. "In the road."

"Totaled the car," Byron interrupted. "So we walked through the woods in the storm. Nothing to guide us but the moon. Which, as you can see, must have been some feat."

"Dang." The guy took a sip, and the song changed to some Euro-pop dance tune that made Jimmy feel nauseous for vaguely cultural reasons. "Anybody get hurt?"

"Yes," Jimmy said.

"No," Byron said.

Jimmy felt Byron stepping on his foot very hard. "Yes and no," he clarified.

Adam's Apple looked oblivious. "Me and my brother have lots of clothes. You want some?"

"We'll give them back to you tomorrow!" Byron replied. "Thanks."

The guy turned toward the living room. "Be right back. Chips and shit are in the kitchen."

"Right," Jimmy muttered under his breath, "we'll give the clothes back. We'll mail them from Manhattan. That's believable."

The kitchen was nearly the size of Jimmy's apartment, with stone floors, granite counters, a percussion orchestra of pots and pans on hooks, and three sinks. "We have to keep our mouths shut, Jimmy. Do you want something to eat?"

"Not if I have to keep my mouth shut."

"God, I love *houses*," Byron said, opening up four cabinets before he found the drinks. "I wish my parents would buy one. Come on, what do you want?"

"Clothes. I can't think until I'm dry." Jimmy turned toward the living room. The music was shaking the house, with speakers placed at perfect angles in all corners of the room. Rugs had been rolled neatly off the floor, which was packed with dancers. Two girls were having jumping contests with full glasses that spilled into puddles on the wood parquet, and three couples were managing to hook up conspicuously on an L-shaped sofa arrangement.

"Your mom never taught you to use an umbrella?" a voice called out.

Jimmy turned to see a boyish-looking girl with short dark hair, green eyes, and wearing a flannel shirt and overalls. "I was in an accident," he said. "We hit a deer."

He turned to go, but the girl's eyes lit up. "Really? Where?"

Jimmy eyed the kitchen. Byron was lost in the crowd. "The highway. About point-six miles away. We were driving here, the three of us—"

"Weird. It's not even hunting season."

"We weren't hunting. We *hit* it—"

The girl laughed. "I know. They get shook up and run all over the place when the season starts. They sense it. That's when a lot of them get killed—zoom, right out into the road. But now, in October? If you want deer meat, it's roadkill or nothing. Do you like venison?"

"What?"

"It's amazing, if you do it right. My dad field-dresses deer. Moose too, but personally, I'm not a fan of moose meat. I have this cousin in Alaska—"

"Uh, excuse me . . . ," Jimmy said, backing into the crowd and looking around desperately for Adam's Apple.

Emerging from a knot of loud frat-boy types was a guy with a shaved head and soul patch. "Duuuuude!" he said, holding up an arm. "Rain Man! Wet T-shirt winner!"

Jimmy let the guy pull him into an obligatory handshake that seemed too forced and obsessively accurate. The guy smelled like Old Spice and had the kind of fussed-over hairline that screamed *old guy losing hair*. "You got anything?" he asked.

"Got?"

"I hear there's some good shit here." The guy winked at him and looked around. "Hey, didn't you come in here with a friend?"

"He's *full* of shit. It's different."

The guy looked confused for a moment, then punched Jimmy on the shoulder. "Funny guy."

Adam's Apple was bounding downstairs now, holding

a bundle of clothes in each hand. After Jimmy's last two encounters, he seemed refreshingly normal. "My bro is about your size," he said, shoving one pile to Jimmy. "Don't tell him I gave you this. Where's your friend?"

"Follow Mr. Clean." Jimmy gestured toward Shaved Head. "Who is that guy anyway, your grandfather?"

"Crasher," Adam's Apple grumbled. "Must have just walked in. Fuck him. You can change in my room. Up the stairs to the left."

"Thanks." Jimmy threaded his way around a kissing couple (oblivious) and three guys playing a game on their iPhones (even more oblivious). At the top of the stairs, a girl screaming, "Eww!" ran past him, abandoning a guy who was kneeling by the toilet (by far the most oblivious).

He turned left and ducked into a room decorated with Korn, AC/DC, and Metallica posters. He sat down on a pile of coats—and it moved.

Jimmy bolted to his feet.

A barely awake face peeked out from beneath the pile. "Do you have Bluetooth?"

"No! Uh, sorry," Jimmy said.

"If we're talking," the guy said with a blissful smile, his eyes closing, "you have Bluetooth. . . ."

Jimmy waited for him to conk out and then quickly

changed clothes into a plaid button-down shirt and khaki pants that came up to his ankles. "Stylin'," he muttered, reaching into the wet pockets of his pants for his wallet and cash. It took him a moment to remember that the phone was gone, but the wallet was soaking wet, so he grabbed a plastic bag from the trash and wrapped it.

Outside the door he could hear Byron talking with someone. He shoved the bag into the pocket of his dry pants and headed for the door.

The music suddenly stopped.

Jimmy heard an agitated murmur of voices, pounding footsteps, a shuffling of furniture, cabinet doors slamming shut, a dozen people *ssshh*ing at once.

Someone poked his head in the door and hissed at Jimmy, "The lights! The lights!"

Jimmy flicked off the switch. The darkness in the room only lasted a moment, as a wash of angry red light came in through the window, sweeping quickly from left to right.

He ran to the window and peered out at a police car parked at the curb, its top light flashing. The happy major-third chime of the doorbell pierced the silence— once, twice . . .

KNOCK-KNOCK-KNOCK-KNOCK!

Now the guy under the coats was sitting up on the bed. "Jenny . . . ?" he said tentatively.

"Sshhh!" Jimmy replied.

The knocking stopped, and an exasperated voice called in through an open window, loud enough to be heard on the second floor:

"Come on, guys, open up. We're just looking for some-body."

Jimmy pushed aside the bedroom curtains and leaned forward for a better look. The policeman had a cell phone in his hand and he was staring at the screen.

"We have a cell phone here registered to someone named Daniel Capitalupo?"

Jimmy instantly fell back from the window at the sound of his father's name.

7

WAITS
October 17, 8:49 P.M.

"So," said Waits, as he leaned into the bar. He faced down a guy with an immaculate baseball cap perfectly positioned backward and pants pulled just-so over the boxer line, an ensemble more JCPenney Fall Spectacular than ghetto. "Remember me?"

The guy did a double take and pretended not to be upset. "Whoa, I didn't recunnize you!" South Shore Long Island, Adam Sandler accent, thick as Manischewitz.

Waits had traded his leather jacket and who-gives-a-fuck wardrobe for an old Brooks Brothers shirt with jeans. Along with the short hair, gelled so that it looked almost black, Waits could have passed for an overworked college poli-sci major coming off a caffeine high. He hated the look, but it almost always took his clients by surprise. Which seemed to be necessary these days. "I gave you credit," he said reasonably, "but not forever."

"Dude. I'm kinda broke."

"You promised me last month."

The guy laughed. "Heyyyyyy . . . what are you, a fuckin' bankuh? Read my lips. I don't have it."

This wasn't cute anymore. He grabbed the guy's shirt with his right hand and pulled the little shitbag close, taking no pleasure in the guy's helpless squeal. With his left hand, in the shadow of the bar but conspicuous enough, Waits pulled out a pocket knife.

Waits tried to flick it open with cool efficiency, but he wasn't too good with pocket knives. So he just held it there for symbolic effect.

"Yo, yo, yo," the guy whimpered. "Can't you take a joke?"

Waits reached into the guy's pocket, lifted his wallet, then pushed him away. The guy's license was right up front in the plastic compartment. These bridge-and-tunnels were proud of their licenses. "Joshua Mil— "

"Hey, that's mine! Give it back. Yo, my dad is a lawyer."

"What's his number? He'll love to hear about his son's Ecstasy habit."

"*What?* It's not my habit. I give the stuff away!"

"Well, I don't, motherfucker." Waits riffled through the wallet. He hated saying *motherfucker*. When he was a student at Olmsted High, he and his friends had always leaned with special brio into the word *motherfucker*, thereby putting ironic verbal quotation marks around it. This was considered a social comment. Stripped of that, the word seemed so artless. "Ninety-three Locust Boulevard . . . area code 516 . . ."

"Asshole." Joshua reached into his pocket and handed Waits a wad of bills, keeping a ten for himself. "So I can get home. Take the rest. You happy now?"

"I'll look forward to the balance tomorrow," Waits said, sticking the wallet in his pocket, "Joshua."

Josh stormed away in a huff.

Watching him go, Waits felt a stabbing pain in his gut. He'd been having a lot of that lately.

"The little prick giving you trouble?" drawled a nasal voice across the bar. Ed the Bartender was a career guy, pushing fifty, with an orange bandanna covering a multitude of baldness and a personal style honed to perfection around August 1979. No one knew his last name, so over time it had defaulted to "the Bartender."

"I hate being a ball breaker," Waits said.

"It doesn't suit your warm and fuzzy personality," Ed the Bartender replied. "What'll it be?"

"Club soda," Waits answered, which elicited the expected horrified gasp from the older man, to which he replied, "Stomach."

"Ouch. You're too young for that shit."

"When did you become my mother?"

"I tried, but I'm too ugly, and my tits are too big." Ed the Bartender shrugged amiably, smacking a glass of club soda down on the bar. "Hey. I feel it too, man. The economy is in Suck Mode. When someone starts squeezing you from above, you have to break balls. Am I right?"

Nodding slightly, Waits took the drink. He wondered if the Mob was rolling Ed the Bartender too. Did he know Ianuzzi?

His gut churned acid at the thought of Salvatore Ianuzzi. Even the club soda hurt going down.

The grinning face, bloated to a waxy sheen by a lifetime of worship at the Church of the Immoderate Consumption, was never far from Waits's thoughts these days. Nor was the unctuous gravel-voice. *Ayyyy, Watts, selling to high school and college is your niche* (the only part worse than the pronunciation of *Waits* as "Watts" being the pronunciation of *niche* as "nitchy")—*it is an investment in the future. They don't pay on time, sometimes they don't pay at all, but that's not the point. They're fuckin' kids—America's future! So we write it off. We grow our database. Build our brand. They come back to us, and they bring their friends. A rising tide lifts all boats.*

It was the same speech every time. And it was total crap.

No one talked about what happened when the tide came in.

Waits leaned against the bar and surveyed the place—a typical Brooklyn mix of hipsters, trustafarians, Wall Street grunts, bridge-and-tunnel puppies—hoping to spot more clients. Everyone was bitching about money these days, just like the nattering heads on the bar TV.

Most of these guys were his age. He'd give anything to be in their shoes now. Even being fired and out on your ass was better than having your life in the hands of Salvatore Ianuzzi.

"Hey, speaking of squeeze, I saw yours yesterday, at Smitty's," Ed the Bartender piped up. He waggled his eyebrows. "Reenie—*rowf, rowf*! She told me she wanted to put a lip lock on my love muscle, but I said she should save herself for you."

"Her name is Reina, she is not my squeeze, no one

even *says* squeeze anymore, she is barely my friend, and fuck you."

Ed the Bartender looked disappointed. "Friend . . . meaning friend with profits?"

"*Benefits*, Grandpa. Not profits. And no."

"But you wish, huh? Admit it. I wouldn't mind getting into her pants, if I could remember how it's done. . . ."

Waits finished his drink and pushed the glass away. He wasn't recognizing any of these faces. And he didn't have the stomach to keep dunning people, or to listen to Ed the Bartender. "Gotta go. Thanks for the superb drinks and conversation."

"Jesus, club soda . . . a guy your age . . ." Ed the Bartender shook his head. "Must be too much sex. It gives you an ulcer."

Waits slapped a twenty on the bar. "Before that last remark, I was going to give you twice as much."

"I can take out my teeth," Ed the Bartender offered cheerfully, "and give you a—"

"Don't finish that sentence!" Waits said with a groan. "You just ruined my day."

As he headed for the entrance, he stopped in his tracks.

There was a funny movement among the mass of

Elvis Costello glasses and bony shoulders. Waits didn't have to see it directly. It was a matter of tectonics, the movement of the bar's human geography to accommodate something that didn't fit. Shoulders the size of an ox yoke.

He was being tailed.

Shit.

Waits changed direction, heading quickly toward the back of the bar. Immediately he heard noises behind him—jostling, the hissing complaints of offended hipsters. He turned briefly. Out of the corner of his eye, he could see an overweight goombah the size of a water tank barreling through the crowd.

Ianuzzi had no sense. In this area of Brooklyn, sending this guy was like dropping an extra from the *Sopranos* onto the set of a Kevin Smith movie.

Waits elbowed his way past the bar crowd, crouching low. As he passed the bathroom, he flipped the door open and then slammed it shut, keeping himself on the outside. It would look like he'd ducked into the john.

Then he slipped into the kitchen through a hanging bedsheet and ran out the back door, into the night.

8

9:04 P.M.

As Waits raced into Prospect Park, Cassie began singing in his pocket.

He was sick of Cassie. He would have to change the ring tone.

He ducked behind the stone wall, peering over. The tail was gone. Quickly silencing the phone, he noticed the name on the screen. Hong. What the fuck did he want now?

"This better be good," he whispered.

"We're on the road," Cam's voice said.

"Is this a fucking field trip? Do I need to give you a permission slip?"

"Dude. That was nasty. I'm just staying in touch."

"Touch my ass. And don't call until you have my

money. And that better be tonight." He paused and added, "Motherfucker."

As he snapped the phone shut, he slipped farther into the park. The sounds of the street were receding. The park was a weird parallel world. In the streets you heard rain from below, the tires sluicing through puddles, the metallic pounding on car hoods. Once you crossed the stone gates, the sonic landscape shifted. Rain pattered overhead on papery leaves. Branches swayed impatiently. You could hear yourself breathe. Footsteps were loud and obvious.

He stuck to the shadows, avoiding the circles of street-lamp light. His breaths rose in agitated wisps as he cut across an access road, jogged over a hill. He glanced over his shoulder again and spotted a couple of silhouettes— two guys, one old and one young. Just hanging out in the pouring rain.

To each his own.

As he angled across a thicket of pine trees, lightning flashed, creating a tesseract of shadows on the ground. Not a good idea to be in the park during a thunderstorm.

Distance from lightning: one mile for each second from the sound of thunder.

One . . . two . . .

He just needed till tomorrow. Then Cam's payment would be in. Pure profit. Waits would give it up to Ianuzzi. They would have a talk. Mano a mano.

Three...

He would tell Ianuzzi how he felt. This life sucked and he wanted out. He'd apologize for losing the tail. Then he'd make a payment plan for whatever was left. And then maybe he could actually talk to Reina and not feel like such a loser.

Four... five...

As the thunder sounded, an arm whipped around from behind him and closed around his neck.

9

9:10 P.M.

"I hate the fuckin' rain," came the voice behind Waits's left ear.

"Achhh... arrrglll..."

The arm was choking him, cutting off air.

"I like snow better. Snow is so pretty in the park. Fuckin' global warming. Do you like snow?"

"Heccchhh..."

Suddenly Waits felt himself spinning, floating. His jaw hit the ground, and he coughed wildly, gulping for air.

"I need... time," Waits said, trying to dig his feet into the ground, anything to gain distance. "Just don't... do anything to me...."

"Yo, what do you think I am, an animal?" the guy said. "Do I look like an animal to you?"

"I'll pay," Waits said. "I promise, dude."

"Yeah, you'll pay." The guy reached inside his jacket.

Shit.

"Don't! *Jesus!*" Waits tried to scramble to his feet.

"Want some gum?" the goon said.

"What?"

"Gum." The guy was holding out a pack of Trident. "G-u-m-m."

"No, thanks."

"Remember that Woody Allen movie where he holds up a bank, only the teller thinks his note says 'I have a gub'? And he calls over all the personnel and they're arguing about what the note really says? It's like, 'gub!' 'No, gun!' 'No, gub!' I love that movie." He laughed, carefully inserting three sticks of gum in his mouth. "Mmmm, they got these tropical flavors now. So, anyway, where was I? Oh yeah, pay up or I rip your fucking fingers out, okay?"

"Okay. I will. Tell Ianuzzi I will."

"He's mad. He says you moved out of your apartment and didn't tell him."

"Privacy issues," Waits said, not wanting to tell the truth: that he wanted to pay what he owed, get out of the business, and cut all ties from Ianuzzi.

"Whatever. He wants fifty."

"*Fifty?* Fifty *grand*? I don't owe him that much—"

"Fifty *percent*. Of what you owe him. Now."

Waits's heartbeat leveled. With the take from Joshua and the cash on hand, he would be relatively close. "I—I think I might have that. Or maybe a little less."

Chewing mightily, the guy made a sad face. "Aw, come on, you have it, right? Please? I hate this fucking job. Especially when I have to work on kids. Ask anyone, does Feets like doing a number on kids? No, he does not."

"Feets? That's your name?"

"Short for Uffizi, like the gallery." The guy's face was like stone. "You come inna my house, you wipe-a Uffizi."

"Uh . . . what?" Waits said weakly.

"Wipe-a *Uffizi*? It's a joke."

"Oh. Okay."

"Christ, no fuckin' sense of humor." Feets leaned closer to Waits, giving off a faint, vaguely rotten odor of fish and rancid olive oil. "You gotta have humor in this business or it kills you."

He was a psychopath. A fish-addled homicidal loony. "Look, I—I'll get the money. When does Ianuzzi want it?"

Feets pulled a small sheet of paper out of his pocket and squinted. "'Simmit's.' I'm supposed to meet you at Simmit's at eleven-thirty."

"Simmit's? You mean, *Smitty's*?"

"Whatever."

"Willard Street?"

"What do I look like, fucking MapQuest? Just be there." The guy crumpled up the sheet and threw it on the ground. As he turned to leave, he let out a sneeze that sounded like a lion's roar. "You know what kind of car Ianuzzi has?"

"A black Cadillac."

"A Hummuh," Feets said, lowering his voice to a religious hush. A pained expression twisted his face, his features muscling awkwardly into an expression Waits took to be a smile. "He has a black Hummuh. I get to drive a black Hummuh. And if you don't watch yusself, you will be going for a ride in the trunk."

10

REINA
October 17, 8:43 P.M.

ru on yr way? its late! u said 8:30.

* SENT 8:43 P.M. 10/17

o shit i 4got sorrrrryyyyy

* cam h RECEIVED 8:49 P.M. 10/17

what do u mean, 4got??????? we were sposed
  to hang tonite!

* SENT 8:50 P.M. 10/17

i 4got i had 2 go 2 this party in wchester. i know i suck.

* cam h RECEIVED 8:52 P.M. 10/17

where ru?

* SENT 8:52 P.M. 10/17

in a car w byron & jimmy

* cam h Received 8:54 P.M. 10/17

ne1 else?

* Sent 8:55 P.M. 10/17

no. like who?

* cam h Received 8:56 P.M. 10/17

like that low-life drug dealer?

* Sent 8:57 P.M. 10/17

f*** wates. i eat him 4 lunch.

* cam h Received 8:59 P.M. 10/17

right.

* Sent 8:59 P.M. 10/17

ru mad at me?

* cam h Received 9:00 P.M. 10/17

cuz the fuckin mets r losing & i cant stand the
    idea of you being mad

* cam h Received 9:01 P.M. 10/17

reina?

* cam h Received 9:03 P.M. 10/17

Reina snapped her phone shut. The popping sound was louder than she expected. It startled her boss, who was getting ready to leave the late shift for her. "Everything all right, babe?"

All right?

All right?

Cam was magic. He was smart and funny, and the best dancer she'd ever known. The way he'd get around his football friends—monosyllabic, crude, and corny—she always figured that was a coping mechanism, boy crap. She could live with two Cams, as long as she got the good one. She hadn't been prepared for the two of them to morph into Mr. Hyde before her eyes.

She began scrubbing the counter with ferocity. "Fine."

"It's that Asian linebacker," said her cousin Gino, sipping a black coffee alone at the deuce near the cash register. "Isn't that an oxymoron? You should never go out with an oxymoron."

"That is a really offensive ethnic stereotype and I can't believe you said it," Reina said.

Gino grinned, springing up from his seat and suddenly vaulting over the counter with the agility that had won him a spot on the Olmsted third-string track team in 1999. She screamed in protest, but he threw his arms around her. "I am an offensive ethnic stereotype and proud of it. Eye-talians on the march! Behold, garlic breath—hhhhhhhhhhh!"

"Stop!" Reina screamed.

Behind them, her boss was chuckling. The two guys

had been friends ever since her boss had coached Gino in CYO baseball back in the nineties. "Break it up, this is bad for business."

"What business? No one's in here!" Gino protested. "Ted, this guy Cam is a turd and deserves to be hung by his short hairs for what he's done to my sweet, innocent, half-breed Puerto Rican cousin, awww, look at da sad widdo puss puss . . ."

Reina threw a Tazo tea bag at him.

"What'd he do this time anyway?" Gino asked.

Reina shrugged. "He was supposed to come here and hang. Listen to tunes. And then after work, we were going to go to the club."

"Club?" Gino looked shocked. "*My* club? Did you clear this with the manager? Do you know how hard it is to get into Blowback?"

"I personally know the manager," Reina said, "and he's a real dick."

"Language, darling . . . ," Ted said, glancing around the empty shop. "This is a family coffee establishment."

"Come anyway," Gino said. "Call another friend. Or come by yourself. Help me run the light show. It's fun."

"I'll think about it," Reina said.

Ted glanced out the door. "You know, it *is* kind of

dead tonight. You probably won't need to stay open the whole time. Tell you what. Shut 'er down at midnight."

Gino rolled his eyes. "Ted, you have a heart of prune."

"I never heard that expression before," the old man said with a laugh, as he put on his silk baseball jacket and wrapped a scarf carefully around his neck. "Like the jacket? I'm thinking of ordering for the entire staff. You'd pay, but I'll keep it close to cost."

"You're cheap, too. I like that in a man." Gino linked arms with Ted and threw a wink toward Reina. "See you after midnight? I'll be there just as soon as I escort Ted to his Senior Singles meeting."

"Eat me," Ted said.

Reina shrugged. "I'll think about it. I may use the time to study for my SATs. Who knows how involved I'll get?"

"Dang, you are one twisted beeyotch," Gino said cheerfully. "See you later!"

As the two walked out, Reina read the back of Ted's jacket:

I ♥ lattes:

They take a latte time

And cost a latte money

But they're worth it!

* Smitty's Brooklyn *
Theodore Smith, Founder

She began cleaning out the espresso machine, vowing she would never, ever wear a jacket like that in her life.

11

BRUNO (AN INTERLUDE)
October 17, 10:57 P.M.

He took at the last drag from a Marlboro and flicked it into the street.

"That is ecologically very destructive to the environment," said Scrotum.

Bruno sat on the steps of the brownstone and held out his pack to the craggy old guy. "Fuck the environment and fuck you. You didn't get so ugly by eating alfalfa sprouts. Want one?"

"I stopped, you little punk," Scrotum said, puffing out his scrawny chest. "I'm old enough to be your grandfather, and I feel like a million bucks."

"You look like forty-nine cents." Bruno put the pack back into his pocket. Suddenly the cigarettes didn't seem like such a pleasurable idea. Being around this guy was a singularly unpleasurable experience. Looking at his face alone, with its saggy jowls, deep lines, bloodshot eyes, and dark thatches of nose and ear hair, was enough to kill anyone's appetite. It was hard to believe he'd passed the exams for the department. Bruno glanced up into the third-floor front apartment across the street. Nothing. No movement.

He knew their mark was there. They'd followed the kid home from Prospect Park, where he'd gotten the shit kicked out of him. Then they'd almost lost him, but Scrotum had gotten the exact address by poking around in the garbage, fishing out a discarded envelope from among the orange peels and sandwich rinds. He was scarily good at that.

The little punk had to come down sooner or later, and until then, he and Scrotum would have to wait. As long as it took. It was a good thing the rain had let up. "So how'd you get the name Scrotum, anyway?"

"It's *Scranton.*"

"Come on . . . how'd you get it?"

The old man looked away. "Guy in the station house. Part-time actor. Was in *The Godfather* or some shit. Did Shakespeare, whatever. One time I come in to the lunchroom, I'm carrying a tray full of sammitches for the guys, he looks up at me and says in this big voice, 'Enter Scrotum, a wrinkled retainer!' " He shrugged. "So . . . it stuck."

Bruno tried to keep from bursting out laughing. "Stuck?"

"Anyways, he told me he didn't make it up. He got it from some Broadway guy."

"The scrotum?"

"The *nickname*, asshole!" He began rolling up his sleeve, revealing a ropy arm and a tattoo, faded and mottled with stretch marks, that said either DOLORES or DORIS.

Bruno jumped off the stoop, cackling, as Scrotum threw an old-school-boxing left jab, which made him laugh even more.

Thunk.

Across the street, the tenement building's iron front door slammed shut. A guy in a black leather jacket and light brown hair, maybe nineteen or twenty—not much younger than Bruno—lifted up his collar as he hurried into the street. He was carrying a hefty shoulder bag and wearing sunglasses.

"That the guy?" Scrotum whispered.

"Get your eyesight checked, Methuselah," Bruno said, leaping to his feet. "Yeah, it is. Let's get moving."

"Whoa . . . whoa . . . don't get too excited," Scrotum said. "We wait a block and keep him in our periphial vision. We gotta let him make the drop—then we take in the big guy. Ianuzzi, the prick. We fuck this up, the chief nails us to the wall."

"Peripheral."

"The fuck?"

"Peripheral. Not periphial." Bruno edged forward, beginning to follow the mark. "There's no such word as 'periphial.'"

"Suck my balls," said Scrotum.

Bruno fought back the image that was edging into his brain.

He never thought police work would be this hard.

12

REINA (RESUMED)
October 17, 11:38 P.M.

Insouciance.

She hated how words popped into her head like that. This had been happening way too much since she'd started taking an SAT prep class, her head crammed with ridiculous words understood by maybe 5.7 percent of the English-speaking world, i.e., a few thousand professors, journalists, and OCD high school kids desperate to get into college. And so it went, all day long: A crying little girl—*lachrymose.* Kids rushing to be on time for class—*celerity.* A door opening into a dark cellar—*tenebrous.* Erasing Cam's text messages—*cathartic.*

And Waits, right there in Smitty's, sitting in a chair where she couldn't help but see him not looking at her, with his leather collar turned up, his sunglasses hiding his eyes, and his face betraying nothing—*insouciance.*

It was the not looking at her that bugged Reina most of all. That and the fact that he'd come in at 11:34, exactly twenty-six minutes before Ted had given her permission to close. She had been looking forward to going to Blowback.

Normally, Smitty's "late crowd" was a bookish, Park Slope-ish bunch who tended to apologize a lot, laugh at odd things, and preface descriptions with "sort of" like a nervous verbal tic. Because they nursed their mocha lattes for hours, she could ignore them and do massive amounts of homework.

With Waits it was a different story. Looking out the window, his black leather shoulder bag tucked under his legs, he angled his cup in her direction. The gesture said *Another double espresso* in an offensively demanding way.

Ted would have jumped at a signal like that from Waits—pour him refills for free, slip him pastries for free. Whenever she'd protest this, he gave her a look that said *Don't fuck with this guy.* Which meant that Ted was just as brainwashed as anyone else. He believed all the legends: Waits had murdered his own parents, he had been kicked out of school for putting cocaine in the water tank, he slept with girls in alphabetical order by their first names, or last names.

All bullshit. Reina didn't buy any of it. Waits was a low-life drifter, an Olmsted head case. Every class had one: The Genius with So Much Promise Who Just Snapped. He didn't deserve all the groveling.

She buried her face in her book, purposefully ignoring him.

Desultory.

"Excuse me?" he said in a voice much sweeter than you would expect—a singer's voice.

Mellifluous.

She looked up, as if just noticing him for the first time. "Hm?"

"Could I have a refill, please?" he asked, glancing at her and then out the window. "If you don't mind."

Deferential.

STOP STOP STOP!

Holding up a finger, she read to the end of the paragraph. It was useless. She couldn't understand a word. With a sigh, she stood and began making the double espresso.

But when she turned to serve him, he had left his

seat. His shoulder bag was gone too. She looked around curiously. Behind her, she heard the sound of running water from the shop's bathroom.

As she placed the steaming cup on the table, the front door opened and two men walked in.

Figured. Just when she needed to pack up, whoopee, happy hour.

The younger guy was almost good-looking, save for a head of slick black hair and an *Ayyyy-babe-if-you're-lucky-I-may-let-you-sleep-with-me* expression. The older guy had basset-hound jowls, canyonlike wrinkles, and arms that looked like deflated balloons. He was flat-out salivating with his eyes, which traveled up and down Reina's body as if he were at a yo-yo tournament. She looked conspicuously at the clock, which read 11:41. "We're about to close."

"It says 'Open till 1:00 A.M.,'" the younger guy protested.

"It's been slow tonight—"

"It's okay," came Waits's voice from behind her.

She turned. Waits was emerging from the bathroom, still buckling his belt. "I think these guys are here to see me," he said insouciantly.

"You?" the older guy said with exaggerated fake surprise. "Never saw you in my life."

Waits gestured for them to sit at his table. "What do you gentlemen want?"

"A venti macchiato half-caf half-decaf with one percent and Equal, no froth?" said the younger guy.

"Small regular coffee, three sugars," mumbled the older guy, who was staring at his partner as if he'd just spoken Norwegian.

"Three sugars?" the younger guy said.

"For my sweet deposition." The older guy shrugged defensively. "What, you don't like that? At least I order in English."

"You fuckin' moron, you have diabetes," the younger one said. "And it's *disposition.*"

Reina turned away and tried to block them out. This wasn't her night.

The two guys seemed somehow thrown by Waits, who, in contrast, was looking very calm. As she focused on her reading, she only picked up occasional snatches of conversation, and more than once the use of the word "scrotum." Nice crowd.

Hoi polloi.

Waits was the first to leave. "Keep the change," he said, slapping a bill on the counter, then bowing slightly to the other two, who did not seem happy. "Gentlemen . . ."

He strolled out the door. The two men stared at the table, not looking up.

Reina pretended to concentrate. *Don't order anything more. Please, don't order anything more. . . .*

Suddenly the older guy pounded the table so hard his cup went flying. *"Shit!"*

He stormed out the door with the younger man in pursuit, leaving the broken cup on the floor and a crumpled five-dollar bill on the table—on a $5.69 check.

With a disgusted sigh, Reina took the money. The clock read 11:59. Right on schedule.

As she grabbed a broom from behind the counter, she noticed a rumpled black shape under the pastry shelf— Waits's shoulder bag. She grabbed it and ran out the door, looking up and down the sidewalk. The street was empty.

Ducking back inside, she flipped the OPEN sign to CLOSED and locked the door from the inside. Time to cash out. Finally. She dropped the shoulder bag behind the counter. It was heavier than she expected, as if it were full of textbooks (yeah, right). Well, he would just have to pick it up tomorrow.

She swept up the broken china, dumped it, bound up the garbage, took the plastic bags outside, and left them on the curb. Ducking back in, she opened the cash register, took the five out her pocket and tucked it into the proper slot, then grabbed the bill Waits had left on the counter.

It was a hundred dollars.

She had to look at it twice. Then she noticed a rumpled napkin next to it, with a message:

KEEP CHANGE. LOCK DOOR, TURN OFF LIGHTS, DON'T MOVE TILL I GET BACK. IGNORE ANYONE WHO COMES BY. -W

What the—?

Reina checked the clock. 12:04. How long did he expect her to stick around? Why the hell couldn't he take his own shoulder bag?

She drummed her fingers on the counter. She could try to track him down, but she really wanted to get to Blowback. She needed the break.

Could he have meant to leave a hundred?

He couldn't have.

She stared at the bag a moment, then lifted it to her shoulder. It smelled of stale cologne. As it plopped back to the floor, the metal zipper slid open a bit and the two halves separated by a fraction of an inch.

Hmm.

She flicked off the outside floodlight and the overhead light, leaving only a dim, pulsing fluorescent behind the counter.

Bending over, she pulled the zipper. The folds of a sweatshirt puffed out of the opening. She slid the zipper the full length and reached inside, pushing away a sweatshirt and a pair of corduroy pants.

Under the pants was a canvas drawstring bag. She glanced to the window again and opened the string.

Hands shaking, she removed a tightly bound stack of bills. Holding them under the light, she riffled through. Hundreds, all of them. In the bag, underneath it, there were at least a dozen more stacks.

Idiot! There would be fingerprints.

Shoving the stack into her pants pocket, she zipped up the shoulder bag. *That* would have her prints too.

Complicit.

Panicked, she reached into her pocket for her cell phone. She could call information. Maybe Waits had a listed number.

As her fingers closed around the phone, it rang.

She fumbled to open it. The screen showed a number she didn't recognize. Probably a pay phone. Guys like Waits still used pay phones. "Hello!" She was shouting now, her voice nearly a screech. "Look, I—I can't—why did you—?"

But the voice at the other end was not Waits. It was vaguely familiar but patching in and out, screaming something about her cousin.

Incomprehensible.

"Who is this?" she shouted.

"Stuck . . . party . . ." the voice crackled. "Help . . . deer . . . Gino . . . Blowback—can we . . . tonight . . . ?"

"Hi! Blowback? You want to meet me there?"

"Yes! . . . Chhhhh . . ."

"Wait, is this—?"

The call sputtered and finally dropped. She was pretty sure the voice belonged to Byron Durgin.

13

BYRON
October 17, 8:59 P.M.

Ouch.

Ouch. Ouch. Ouch.

All the major indexes, down the toilet. Again. Hang Seng, NASDAQ, Nikkei bleak-ay.

Byron was not happy. He glanced away from his BlackBerry. Looking at the screen while the car was moving made him feel nauseated. Which made the sucky news even suckier.

He tried not to think about it. How could *all* his market guesses have been so dead wrong? When you lost this big, it was embarrassing. When you lost this big with other people's money, you made headlines. Financial Whiz Kid Takes Investors to Cleaners. You kissed college good-bye.

You looked forward to the kind of life laid out in countless cautionary movies. Exile to Las Vegas. Addiction. Abandonment. Homicide. If you were lucky, Philip Seymour Hoffman played you and died in a pool of vomit.

Worse, he would be just another fucked-up Durgin, following in the footsteps of five brothers and a sister in various stages of genetically predetermined failure. His dad was going to kill him. *The kid is perfect*, Sergeant Durgin loved to say. *Either a genetic mutant or we're just waiting for the other shoe to drop.*

Ha-ha.

Thump.

Byron tried to focus on the trees outside, blurred by the rain and speed. It just made him feel worse.

The whole world should be connected by subway, he thought. On the subway, he never got nauseated. He wasn't suited for car travel. Or the suburbs. Or losing.

Especially losing.

"AWWWW, NO WAAAAAYYY!" In the front seat, Cam was spazzing out over a baseball game on the radio, at the same time that he was texting on his cell phone.

And Byron once again couldn't believe that he was here—getting involved in this stupid kind of scheme—with a guy who could get so worked up over a team of nine steroidal total strangers. "It's only a game," Byron said. "These guys don't give a shit about you."

"Oh, and you don't get all mental over the market, do you?" Cam shot back. "At least when the game is over, nobody goes broke."

Byron sighed. For the twentieth time since getting into the car, he felt in his pocket for the envelope. The heft of it, the shifting of the merchandise inside it as he moved around, was reassuring and scary as hell.

Easiest cash we'll ever make, Cam had said.

Which alone was enough to run the other way. But when the other way was a corner, when your portfolio was underwater and you owed five hundred to pay a margin call, you took a chance. You did your own version of what the queen was purported to do when getting laid. Lie back, close your eyes, and think of England.

"Friggin' Mets!" Cam pounded the dashboard. "Can you believe that shit? Can you *believe* it? Hit-and-run with one out at the top of the ninth—I mean, what were they thinking?"

"Unbelievable," Jimmy agreed, gripping the steering wheel tightly, leaning forward. It was pouring and the road must have been slippery, but he drove like an old lady.

Jimmy could be annoying.

Byron looked at the back of his head in disbelief. "Tell us, James, what's so fucking unbelievable about it? Did you even understand what happened?"

"I could crash this car so easily if you don't stop distracting me," Jimmy murmured.

"Sorry," Byron replied.

Jimmy glanced over his shoulder. "What are you so pissy about all of a sudden?"

The radio announcer was blathering on, his staccato voice competing with the static: *The management is insisting that trade rumors for a third basemen are untrue, as Delgado steps up to bat . . .*

Cam, done with his texting, was now talking to someone on his phone.

"I'll tell you why I'm pissy," Byron said, slipping his BlackBerry into his pocket. "Sports announcers. The butchers of the English language. 'As'? Did you ever notice the way they use 'as'? I mean, they're talking about one thing and then it's like, oh, whoops, I forgot I'm supposed to be calling the game, so I'll just stick an 'as' in there, for that sophisticated and silky-smooth transition. *'Today Osama bin Laden was captured while humping his favorite goat, as Martinez throws a fastball for a strike . . .'*"

Jimmy's head was arranged like a question mark.

Cam shifted around, his massive shoulders crowding the space between the seat and the dashboard. "That time of the month, Shirley?"

"Fuck you," Byron said.

This car was a big What's-Wrong-with-This scenario: Jimmy the Worrywart driving, Byron the Broke carrying the goods, and Cam serving as the brains of the operation. Cam, the star player for the Olmsted Architects, a football team every bit as pathetic as you'd expect from a high school where a 2099 SAT score put you in the bottom half of the class.

Cam pushed his seat back, jamming Byron's legs. Byron responded by kneeing the back of Cam's seat. "Mm, that felt kind of nice," Cam said, "*as* I feel a little tingle in my groin, *as* we get closer to the party."

"As Byron Durgin leans forward and says, once again, fuck you," Byron said.

"Name the date, sweetie."

Now Cam was scanning the radio stations. "*This in from Metro-North—all trains in and out of Grand Central are canceled due to storm-related electrical failure. Express buses will be picking up outbound passengers at the following locations . . .*"

"Dang. Glad we're in a car," Jimmy said.

"Too bad the Mets aren't playing at home," Cam grumbled. "A rainout's better than a loss."

He kept his finger on the SCAN button and stopped at a country station—"WMLT, Mullet Radio, Westchester's country station!" the DJ bellowed. "With our country countdown—*nnnnnnumber one!*"

"No. Absolutely not," Byron said. "Shoot that radio."

"Yee-HAH!" Cam hooted as a twangy intro began. "I love this song—it's about some hungover dude. He's so shitfaced, he checks the obituaries for his own name. . . ." He began singing along, loud and tunelessly. "*Well, Ah'm drinkin' down coffee but coughin' up beer! Ah'm checkin' t'see if Ah'm still here . . .*"

Byron howled. "Aggh! Stop! You'll break the windows!"

"Will you guys knock it off!" Jimmy shouted. "I can't even see the goddamn road!"

The GPS device, which had been silent for a while, chimed in: "In point-six miles, turn right and go to the end of the road . . ."

That was the last thing Byron heard before he spotted the sudden movement on the side of the road, out of the woods and into the light.

14

9:09 P.M.

Byron had to blink a dozen times, each time hoping the dream would end. But the unreal was real. Jimmy was standing outside in the rain, the car was at a precarious slant, glass was strewn over the backseat, and a deer was lying across the front seat.

Kicking.

"Jesus," Byron blurted out, "it's still alive!"

"N-n-no shit . . ." came Jimmy's voice.

The envelope.

Byron felt in his right pocket. He had fallen on that side of his body, so the envelope had been shielded from the rain that was pouring in sideways through the broken windshield. He fingered the opening and reached inside. The stuff was still wrapped in plastic. Intact.

Now what?

A crash meant cops.

Shit. This was Jimmy's fault. *How could Jimmy let this happen?*

He was yelling shit at Jimmy. His mouth was going of its own will. Soon he was outside the car too, his hands grabbing the guy's phone, preventing him from doing the stupidest possible thing: calling the cops. Byron's mind was in warp mode, rearranging the reality into an impossibly fucked-up knot. The plan was shot to shit, he had possession, his own BlackBerry was dead, Jimmy was a useless mess, and . . .

Cam.

Holy shit. Cam was under the deer.

How could he have forgotten Cam? Why was Jimmy just standing there?

Leverage. He'd need a rope.

As he raced to the trunk, shouting instructions to Jimmy, the envelope felt like it weighed a hundred pounds. He glanced out to the woods.

Fling it away.

Great. The squirrels would be happy beyond their wildest dreams, but Byron would come home empty-handed, unable to pay Waits back, and next week they'd be pulling his ass out of a swamp in Red Hook.

Swallow it.

Um, no.

Stick it up—

Not even going there.

He flung open the trunk. Despite the damage, the light was working. Inside were the usual supplies—antifreeze, windshield fluid, paper towels, empty beer cans, flashlight, blanket, crowbar. . . .

There.

The rope was perfect, a long, thick, braided cable. He grabbed it and the flashlight, and ran around the car. Jimmy was staring at him through the windshield, with a look that projected admiration, disbelief, and abject fear.

But Jimmy would obey. Jimmy yielded to the alpha dog. That was the good thing about Jimmy.

The deer now motionless, Byron went to work. He wrapped one end of the rope around the narrowest part of the deer's legs, the other around the nearest tree.

Stepping back, he watched hopefully as Jimmy floored the gas pedal. After a few attempts, the thing finally slipped off—and Jimmy went skidding back, smacking into a guard rail.

Byron raced over to him. "Are you okay?"

"Fah—fah—" Jimmy stammered. He was shaken but intact.

Byron shone the flashlight into the passenger side. Cam, unfortunately, did not look so great. He was soaked in blood, his eyes shut and his arm hanging in a funny way. Byron tried to make out any movement in Cam's chest, but his own hands were shaking. Was he dead? *He couldn't be dead.*

The rain seemed to pick up, making hollow noises against the hood, tinkling against the piles of glass. And in the distance, a siren sounded.

Byron drew back, shutting the flashlight. "Shit! Did you call them?"

"No!" Jimmy said.

"Then how do they know?"

"Someone drove past us, just after the accident. Maybe they called."

Byron's stomach clenched. "Someone saw us?"

"This is a New York suburb. Occasionally people drive on the roads."

Drug trafficking. Unlicensed driving. Manslaughter.

"Oh, God. Oh, God. Oh, God. Oh, shit. Oh, God."

Byron backpedaled. He reached into his pocket, grabbing the envelope.

Run.

No. He couldn't leave Jimmy. And how suspicious would that be, anyway? Jimmy didn't know anything, but cops could connect the dots.

He'd have to take Jimmy with him. But he'd have to hide the stuff first. If the cops found him and Jimmy, they would have to be clean. Later they could come back for it. He looked around frantically for a hiding place.

The bushes. Too wet and too obvious. *A knot in a tree.* Too hard to find. *The car?* Oh, sure, and leave an unexpected treat for the night-shift mechanics.

The siren was growing louder. They had to leave. Jimmy was in the car, sobbing, trying to revive Cam. Byron backed away, shaking. The siren was growing louder.

Byron's leg hit against the deer, and he jumped away. The beast was distended and misshapen now, its back curved the wrong way and its head tilted upward. Its eyes were staring and its mouth, small and tight, was open wide as if it were ravenous for something to eat.

It wouldn't be swallowing anything now.

Lightning cracked overhead, momentarily making the deer's face an anguished rictus.

There.

It was the perfect place. And the thought of it made Byron's stomach turn inside out.

He looked away for a moment, fishing the envelope out of his pocket.

Then, holding his breath, he inserted it into the deer's mouth. The tongue was still warm. And bloody.

Leaning over a nearby bush, he retched.

15

10:22 P.M.

"If I . . . close my eyes . . ."

It felt good to hear music. It felt good to be indoors. It felt good to have found a bottle of single-malt Scotch hidden away in the kitchen cupboard. After the walk through the woods, he had been shivery and tense.

The living room was jumping to a dance tune everyone seemed to know. Byron had somehow lost Jimmy. He wandered up the stairs, dry clothes in hand, trying not to disturb the various gropings along the stairway. Mouths jabbering, mouths kissing, mouths tonguing. Mouths, mouths, mouths, mouths . . .

He slipped on a step and rammed into one of the couples.

"Owww!" The guy spun around, revealing a mouthful

of orthodonture and blood, an image that was far too close after tonight's events.

"Sorry," Byron drawled.

Coffee. He needed a cup of coffee. Drinking straight from the bottle of Lagavulin had not been a good idea on an empty stomach. At the time he thought it might ease the pain, stanch the flow of images. Cam . . . the deer . . . it was one or the other, wherever he looked—behind the sofa, out the kitchen window, behind the closet door left ajar, anywhere there was a patch of darkness.

The bloody-mouthed couple was glaring at him. Everyone was staring at him. Did they know what happened? Did they know that he had run from the scene of a crime? Had the accident been on the news? Byron Durgin, the Fallen Genius. *His father, a retired New York City cop, urged his son to give himself up and join the family pantheon of losers.*

No. He couldn't lose it. He had to hang on. This was salvageable.

He would somehow return to the deer and find what he needed. And after that, come back to the party. His fifty percent was a hundred, now that Cam was—

Byron stopped at the top of the stairs, gripping the newel post. He felt ill. How could he be thinking about

Cam's percentage? He should donate it. To charity. To Cam's family. For the funeral.

"Yo, um? Are you okay?" asked some girl, sitting on the stairs, who had a diagonal swath of dyed emo black hair. "'Cause if you're about to yack, the bathroom's on the left? I've had enough of guys yacking their brains out?"

"I'll get back to you on that." Byron marched to the top of the stairs and ducked into the first room he saw, directly in front of him.

It was a girl's room, neat, decorated with stuffed things everywhere. He flicked on the light, hoping Jimmy would already be there, but the only occupants were a couple on the bed, writhing and giggling. They didn't seem to care that Byron had entered.

Shielding himself behind an armchair, he let his wet clothes drop to the floor and changed into the dry outfit. The T-shirt was skintight, the sweatpants rose above his ankle. He'd need to take his wallet and dead BlackBerry, but the sweatpants had no pockets, nothing to carry them in. He looked around for another pair of pants, a jacket, a fanny pack, *something* he could use.

On the bed, the girl was peering out from under her boyfriend. "'My parents went to the Minneapolis Skyway and all they brought me was this T-shirt'? Cute."

Byron cringed, instinctively covering up the slogan on his shirt. He grabbed someone's jacket off the floor and put it on, only to discover it wasn't a jacket. It was a thick cotton robe.

Quickly gathering up his stuff, Byron bolted through the door—and ran smack into an older guy with a shaved head. "Whoa!" the guy shouted, looking at the bundled clothes in horror. "What'd you do, piss yourself?"

"Sorry, wardrobe malfunction," Byron said. "It's just water, dude."

"Heyyyy, you're the guy Angus told me about—came in from the rain—stalled car, right?"

"Angus?" Byron said.

"Give 'em to me. I'll wash these babies for you." The guy snatched the clothes from Byron's arms and headed downstairs.

"Hey, wait, I need—"

"They'll be dry in no time!"

"*—I need the stuff from my pants pockets!*"

The guy stopped on the stairs, surrounded by other kids who were staring at the commotion. He turned with a look of embarrassed contrition and gave Byron the BlackBerry and wallet. "Whoops. Sorry about that."

"What are you, the houseboy?" Byron murmured as

the guy bounded away. *Washing clothes, in the middle of a party?*

Instinctively he counted the money.

Emo Girl was still sitting at the top of the stairs. She looked at him with probing eyes. "You were smart. Your cell phone, your wallet—he already had them in his hand when you asked for them. He dug them out of your pocket."

"Who is he?" Byron demanded.

"Who do you think?" the girl said as if even asking the question wearied her unnecessarily.

Byron ran downstairs and scanned the room. The guy was nowhere to be seen. His heart was racing. What kind of party *was* this?

Chill. . . . Think this through. Okay. Some lowlife thief. Big deal. The guy went away with nothing but some wet clothes. The worst had been averted. Byron had to get the fuck out of here, now. He had to find the deer, retrieve the stuff, and get back ASAP.

He ran toward the back of the house. Outside it looked as if the rain had let up. Halle-fucking-lujah. It shouldn't be too hard to find the accident site if he used the road instead of the woods. The question was, how far away was it? He had no clue.

The back exit led onto a long, screened-in porch. The lights were out, but he could make out a door at the far end. His footsteps thumped dully on the plank floor.

As he reached for the latch, a voice called out to him: "Cam?"

Byron spun around. A guy with slicked-back hair approached with a sly grin. He was holding an unlit cigarette. "Like the robe."

"It's not mine," Byron said. "I borrowed it."

"You don't look the way I expected you to," the guy said, his eyes flickering nervously past Byron into the house.

"Um, actually, that's because I'm—," Byron stammered.

"I'm Frazer," the guy said. "I live here. Angus's brother? You didn't answer my last text message, Cam."

"Well, I—that wasn't . . . um, what *was* the message?"

Frazer pulled out a lighter and offered Byron a cigarette. "Basically, dude, I was saying that if you show up here, you're a fucking dead man."

16

"Dead man?"

The guy was moving closer, eyeing him in a creepy way.

"I figured by now they'd be dragging you out the front door in chains," Frazer said. "They're crawling all over this place."

"Uh, I'm kind of new to this, Frazer. Pretend you're talking to someone who knows only Swedish. Define 'they.'"

"You know, the dudes old enough to be my uncles?" Frazer whispered. "You *did* notice them. I mean, they're like, *My peeps! Rad! Far out!,* with their balding heads and beer guts. They think we're so fucking stupid we can't tell."

Byron nodded, his heart thrumming. "But why—?"

"*Narcs*, dude," Frazer said. "What are you, like, home-schooled or something? *Narcs.* Someone tipped them off."

Okay. This made perfect sense. "He—the cop—tried to take my cell phone."

"They wanted your contact list. The dicks."

"It's broken anyway. . . ."

"They can fix it."

"Who could have tipped them off?"

Frazer cocked his head. "You got any enemies here in Westchester, Cam?"

Byron's brain was spinning. *You hold the stuff,* Cam had said. *You're the one who needs the money.*

Could Cam have been leading them into a trap?

"I have to get out of here," Byron said.

"Duh," Frazer replied.

"Listen, Frazer, my man. I am totally fucked with transportation. My car—it's totaled. You saw the way I was, all soaked when I came in. A deer jumped out. I didn't see it. Huge mother—"

DING-DONG!

The doorbell made them both turn. From inside the house, there was a scream. A sudden hush. Racing footsteps.

Frazer went pale. He grabbed Byron's arm and shoved him out the back screen door.

"Who's at the front door?" Byron said, stumbling down the steps and nearly falling on his face.

"Those douche bags have got undercover guys here already—why the fuck are they raiding the place?" Frazer replied, pulling Byron across a wide, rain-soaked backyard. "We're clean. It's like a sixth-grade graduation party in there. Maybe one of the plainclothes guys planted something—"

"The cops are at the door? The real cops?"

Frazer frowned, his nostrils flaring. "Shit. You were drinking. I can smell it."

"There was Scotch—"

"In the kitchen. Fuck. Dad's single malt. Forgot about that."

The house had fallen silent, and Byron could hear a deep voice calling out a name. Daniel or Emmanuel or something.

"Maybe just a noise complaint, who knows?" Frazer said. "But whatever it is, get your ass away from my house. Now."

"I love you too. But it's a long way back to the Upper West Side."

Frazer dug into his pocket and tossed him a set of keys. "The middle car. Silver. It's got satellite alarm systems that will track you to Mars, so don't get any ideas. Bring it back tomorrow before my mom and dad get back from Gstaad. Like, two o'clock."

"Thanks," Byron said. As Frazer jogged back to the house, Byron stared at the keys in his hands and for the first time in his life cursed the fact that he had grown up in New York City.

He needed Jimmy to drive. Which meant Jimmy would have to take him to the deer, and sit there while he retrieved the envelope from its mouth. Which meant Jimmy would have to know.

He'd hoped to avoid this, but what the fuck. They were both in this up to their kishkes now.

He turned back toward the house. It was dark and silent. He had read in *New York* magazine about what happened when parties got busted in Westchester. It was like a venerated game—hide the booze, flush the dope, nuke the noise, and lay low until the cops lose interest. An arrangement made necessary by the idea that any busted head might belong to the son of a Fortune 500 macher with enough political clout to Roto-Root the entire local civil service structure.

As he got closer, though, lights began flickering on. A commotion had started inside the living room. Kids were clumping together in the kitchen and the porch to watch. He snuck inside and made his way through the muttering groups, scanning the faces for Jimmy.

In the kitchen doorway he took his place next to a girl and a guy gazing into the living room, clutching each other as if having just heard that the nukes had been launched at Westchester, or worse, John Mayer had died.

A uniformed cop was clomping down the stairs into the living room. Behind him was another cop.

Handcuffed to him, and weeping, was Jimmy Capitalupo.

17

10:46 P.M.

Key: Lincoln. Car: Lincoln. It all checked out. No other Lincoln in the garage. This had to be right.

Once again Byron tried turning the key in the ignition. It wouldn't budge.

This was not how things happened in his dad's car. That one *started* when you turned the fucking key.

He hit the horn by accident. He banged the steering column. He tried to move the shift. The sleeve of his robe caught on the shift and pulled it to neutral. He stepped on the accelerator. He stepped on the brake.

VRRROOOMMMMMM! The engine echoed through the garage. Byron nearly screamed.

He breathed deeply, slowly. He tried to remember the lessons his dad had given him the past summer in

Vermont . . . in a parking lot . . . on a dirt road. . . . He tried to blot out the part where he'd plowed into a mailbox.

Voices screamed inside his head: *Why were the cops after Jimmy? How could they have possibly traced him to this house? If they wanted him, did they want me, too?* Jimmy would tell them. Jimmy would break down crying and give them a description right down to the number of pimples on Byron's face.

Concentrate. Pull it together.

He started flicking things, looking for the light switch. The left turn signal flashed. Water sprayed onto the windshield. The wipers wiped. The doors locked. The doors unlocked. The hood popped open an inch.

Finally he found the switch and the garage erupted in bright light. Calmly, he stepped on the brake, slipped into reverse, and stepped on the gas.

RRRRRROMMMMMM . . .

The car tore out of the garage backward, tires squealing. The edge of the house loomed closer in the rearview mirror. Byron yanked the steering wheel the other way. The car rocked, skidding back on the driveway. He slammed on the brake to avoid a tree and found himself diagonal on a small basketball court.

Oops.

"Nice," someone yelled from behind a bush.

"You killed a squirrel," someone else said.

Byron caught his breath. Steam wisped from the hood—and beyond it, he could see the road.

The gearshift gave him a choice of 1, 2, 3, 4, and D. He shifted to 1, gave it gas, and nosed down the driveway.

And they're off.

The car inched forward. Model T speed. A few minutes later, he thumped over the lip of the driveway onto the road. He turned in the direction they'd come, from the left. He edged into the lane. A pair of headlights suddenly glared at him from the other direction, coming closer, fast.

"Aaaagh!" He turned the steering wheel to the right, bouncing up onto a shoulder, steered back into the road, and just missed a head-on collision.

"You fucking drunk, get off the road!" a voice bellowed as the other car whizzed past, honking loudly.

Byron threw him the finger and steadied the car.

Another car passed. Second gear, then third. Twenty-five miles an hour . . . thirty . . . thirty-five . . .

He kept his eye on the left side of the road for the deer. How far away had they been? It was impossible to tell.

Not too far ahead, a red pickup had pulled over to the

opposite shoulder. Someone wearing a bomber hat and a red-checked hunting jacket was loading something onto the rear. Byron pressed the brakes to slow down.

HONNNNNK! Behind him, an Expedition was flashing its brights, then roaring past him on the left.

Byron gulped, glancing back into his rearview mirror.

He was past the pickup, and now he could see exactly what the person was loading onto the flatbed.

A very large, very dead deer.

18

11:01 P.M.

Byron slammed on the brake.

EEEEEE . . .

He hated driving this fast. If you moved the steering wheel just a little bit, you went swerving like a maniac.

The guy was getting into the pickup now, pulling away.

Who the fuck picked up roadkill and brought it home?

Maybe this was how they hunted in Westchester, New York. Maybe it saved the hassle of actually getting a gun permit, of having to spend hours in the woods. Country living without the muss and fuss.

It wasn't long before the pickup had sped out of sight. Luckily it left tracks in the rain, easy to follow, and no one else was on the road to mess them up. The road became hilly after a couple of miles, and the tracks turned up into a narrow gravel road cut into the woods. He followed the road as it wound past a swollen stream. Ahead of him, he could see a clearing and a light. He heard a distant door slam.

Quickly he shut off his headlights and pulled over.

Stopping the car was a lot easier than starting it. He closed his door silently and tiptoed the rest of the way.

Before long the stream's roiling sound gave way to a more placid, controlled splashing just ahead of him. Through the night air he detected the cozy warm scent of a wood-burning fireplace. He edged along farther, following the road as it veered off to the right, into a clearing. And he realized the long winding road hadn't been a road at all.

It was a driveway.

At its end, the path widened. Lit by low, mushroom-shaped lights, it circled around a vast manicured lawn. In the center of the lawn was a giant marble fountain with a winged statue. Just beyond, at the top of a small rise, a sprawling, colonnaded brick mansion loomed over the grounds.

Byron ducked behind a bush and peered carefully over the top. Near the house, the driveway forked. Its right-hand path disappeared into darkness, broken only by the glint from a pair of reflectors.

Keeping to the underbrush, he walked closer to the source of the reflection—the rear lights of the pickup. It was parked in front of a much smaller house that stood a short distance away from the mansion.

He eyed the flatbed intently. He could see the curve of the deer's furry flank peeking over the top. Good.

He figured he had about thirty yards. If he was quiet enough, if he stayed in the brush until the last possible moment, this could work. The wetness of the ground helped muffle sound. All around him raindrops fell from branches, making soft *plup-plup*s on the fallen leaves.

When he was close, he stepped out of the woods. He padded softly over the gravel. Now he could see the deer's face. The slightest hint of something white inside its mouth.

He fought back the revulsion in his gut, the odd tastes that were beginning to well up from his stomach. *Take it. Take it and go.*

As he reached in, he heard a sudden sharp click.

"What do you think you're doing?" came a voice from behind him.

Byron spun around to face down the barrel of a shotgun.

19

11:20 P.M.

"Th—that's my d-deer!"

The words sounded stupid the moment they emerged from Byron's lips.

At the other end of the shotgun, the eyes crinkled. *"Your deer?"*

"Well, not *mine*, but—"

"Do you have a license for this deer? Does it answer to a name? It's eleven o'clock at night, you perv. Why were you following me in your bathrobe?"

The eyelashes, the voice, the stubble-free face—they didn't belong to a he, Byron realized. "I—I thought you were a guy."

"Whatever floats your boat, sweetie," she replied. "Sorry to disappoint, but—"

"I didn't mean that! I meant I wasn't following *you*. I want the deer!"

Her eyes widened. "Oh, that is sick. That is just *too* sick—"

"*Would you put that thing down and let me talk*? Just give me two seconds. I need something . . . *inside* the deer. I put it there. In the mouth."

She lowered the gun, a smile growing across her face. "You put something in its mouth?"

"Two seconds. Please."

"You put something in the mouth of dead deer . . . *and then left*? What was it?"

"I—I had to hide something from cops, okay? There was an accident—"

The girl's eyes widened. "Ohhhh. So you were involved in that, too. I met your friend at that party. Was it something you were bringing—like alcohol?"

"No!"

She glanced at the deer's mouth, leaning closer. "That looks like an envelope . . . *drugs*?"

God, he hated her guts. "Look, this is none of your business."

"Ha! That is *so* straight-to-DVD!" She leaned over the back of the truck.

"Let me do it! You can get . . . rabies!"

Byron tried to run ahead of her, but she blocked his path with the barrel of the rifle. "Uh-uh-uh. I'm from a place where we put the Second Amendment first, dude. You know, that big empty field that stretches from the Hudson River to the edge of L.A.? We know something about sticking our hands inside livestock, Yankee."

She placed the rifle down into the flatbed and used both hands to pull open the deer's jaw. Byron lunged after her but she reached in, yanked out the envelope, sprang back, and held it high. "What'll you give me for it?"

"Come on, this isn't a game!"

Byron swiped for it, but she pulled it away with a teasing smile. "You're from the city, aren't you?" she said. "You know how I figured it out? You're a really bad driver. You nearly spun off the road three times. Anyone your age who can't drive has to be from the city. Am I right?"

"GODDAMN IT, GIVE ME THAT ENVELOPE!"

"Shhhhh. The massuh be sleepin'. Grabbing him by the arm, she pulled him farther away from the house, back in the direction he'd come from. "He don' like it when de slabe chillun be socializin' pas' dawk and takin' de Lawd's name in vain."

"That is so fucking racist and not funny," Byron said.

"Who are you anyway? You live in this house?"

"The little one, not the big one," she said. "With my dad. He works in the big house, for this Wall Street couple. We never see them. Dad calls them Mr. and Mrs. Paycheck. We're from North Dakota originally. You can call me MC. For Mountain Chick. So, where in the city do you live? SoHo? Tribeca? NoLita? Alphabet City?"

"Is this Twenty Questions? The Upper West Side, okay? Now give me the envelope!" He lunged, but she was lithe and fast.

"Do you know East? The club?"

"No!"

"Then why should I give this back to you?"

"*What's the point?*" Byron shouted. *"How do those things connect?"*

"In case you haven't noticed, I am in the power seat, dude," MC said with a cocky smile. "Possession, in cases such as this, is ownership. So, your fate is in my little hands, and all because I thought this head would look good on our mantelpiece."

"It doesn't have antlers. You can't mount it if it doesn't have antlers."

"Says who? That is so sexist. Female deer are worthy of display too."

"I thought you were from Second Amendment land, anyway. You *shoot* the damn things, you don't pick up roadkill."

MC shrugged. "It's about time management. So, you don't go to any clubs at all?"

Byron rubbed his forehead. She was out of her mind. *Play along.* "I—well, sometimes. I know somebody whose cousin runs one of the clubs. Down by the Meatpacking District."

Her eyes widened. "No. Which one?"

"Blowback, okay?" Byron said.

"*No-o-o-o* . . . ," MC said, the word drawn out into a disbelieving gasp. "*Blowback*? Where Madonna and Leonardo go? And Idina and Taye? You can get in there?"

"Sure. Yeah. Whatever. Anytime." This was beginning to make his stomach curdle. "Look, you win. I don't drive too well, and the car isn't mine. I have to return it and I'm scared to get back in. I was supposed to sell this—*that*, what you're holding—at this party, but the guy who drove us there totaled the car. Hence the deer. I'm pretty sure he's dead, too, but my other friend and I ran away. We chickened out and watched the EMT guys take away the body. On top of all this, I . . . I need to pay somebody back, big-time. I thought I could go back to the party but there are cops all over it."

What was happening to him? For the first time all night, he felt tears welling up in his eyes. He fought them back fiercely. She was the last person he wanted to see that.

"Look, Cam was—is—*was*—my friend. I have to repay, for his sake, at least."

"Wow, no wonder you're such a mess. . . ." MC said softly. "Hey, if you can get into Blowback, you can solve your money problems. That's all people do there, buy drugs."

"Thanks." Byron nodded. He hated, *hated* the fact that what she had just mentioned actually seemed like a good idea. "Okay, look, all I'm asking is for you to give me the envelope so I can go back to the city."

"How would you get there? It's like two miles to the train station."

Byron sighed. "Could you drop me off? You could use the Lincoln. Then you wouldn't even have the gas expense."

"And I could return it to the party for you," she said.

"You would . . . do that?"

"Depends," she said with a coy smile. "What do I get in return?"

Byron thought about this. He was going to give Cam fifty percent anyway, so giving her something wouldn't be unreasonable. "Okay, you found the deer, so I'll give you a . . . finder's fee. Ten percent of whatever I sell."

"Fifty-fifty," the girl said.

"*Half?* What are you, nuts?"

MC glared at him with disgust. "You just told me your friend died. So you're—you're planning to skim off his percentage? Is that it? Profiting from . . . from *that*? That is despicable. Don't tell me you were only going to pay him ten percent!"

She tucked the envelope into her jacket pocket and headed to the pickup. "Wait!" Byron blurted. "Twenty-five!"

"I think you are lowballing me," she said, lifting the shotgun out of the flatbed, "I could, of course, cancel the whole deal and take this envelope to the cops."

Byron felt himself shriveling up inside. "Okay, okay. Fifty-fifty."

"Was that the deal with your friend?" she asked warily.

"Yes," Byron said, too tired to unpack how absurd and morbid this line of reasoning was.

The girl pumped her fist. With a giggle, she turned

and ran toward the house. "Stay here. I need to change. And you need to lose that robe. I'll bring you some clothes too. You're about my dad's size."

"Change for what?" Byron shouted.

She turned, with a beaming smile. "We're going clubbing."

As she disappeared into the darkness, Byron felt his knees give way. He sat on the bumper of the pickup. The deer seemed to be eyeing him over it own flanks.

"Fuck you, too," he muttered.

Dzzzzt.

A sudden vibration in his robe pocket made him jump. It took him a moment to realize it was his Black-Berry.

It was working again.

He snatched it and looked at the screen. Nothing, just spam in his in-box.

Glancing over his shoulder, he began tapping out a number.

PART TWO
BEFORE AND AFTER

20

WAITS BEFORE
October 16, 4:07 P.M.

Go ahead, child, make your eyes narrow—that's it, just like mine. Did all those apartment buildings go away? Bravo. Now. Can you see it? Look hard. Can you see me?

Waits squinted. Even now. It was a habit.

On a foggy day in Eisenhower Park, he always thought about Iz. His great-grandfather had died years ago, but Waits could still feel the skin of his palms, cold and papery. The old guy had lost his eyesight, but when he took Waits's hand they saw everything together—steamships coming into New York Harbor in 1924, immigrants gathered on deck before the Statue of Liberty. And, of course, the little boy Isadore at the edge of the ship's railing, leaning over the sea in search of "dollah bills" floating in the sea.

I see him, Iz! I see him!

'Atta boy, little fella. See, that's the magic!

"Yo, yo, yo, yo—Waits, my *man!*" a voice blurted out behind him.

Fade to black. Back to business as usual.

He knew this voice: the pimply sophomore from Far Rockaway. Owed twenty-five dollars from last May. Big on apologies and promises, short on cash. "Fuck you," Waits said without turning.

"I'm just *sayin'.* Next *week,* dude."

"What part of 'fuck you' don't you understand?"

He felt for them. He'd been one of them. You couldn't be going to Olmsted and not be a little nuts. The odds of getting in—top 800 scorers out of 25,000 applicants— were worse than Harvard. And then you faced a four-year battle with man-eating gladiator geeks who stacked the competition so bad that anything less than triple-800/98 GPAs could mean state school. The stress-outs were famous. Every few years they merited an article in *Time* or *Newsweek* and continued to be the basis for steady income to an army of local shrinks. But parents loved the Olmsted cachet, so rather than send their poopsies to another school, they cajoled diagnoses. They paid consultants.

Waits had been there. Actually, he'd loved the Big O

for the first two years, until his dad left the family to live in France with a flight attendant named Pierre. Somehow that seemed to knock things off track. Waits began seeing a few consultants of his own, for pain management.

And now the students consulted Waits.

Which was why he was here, a few yards away from the school building, a few minutes before the end of eighth period. Staring out over the Hudson, remembering.

Can you see it? Look hard. Can you see me?

It wasn't working today. On the other shore, the New Jersey condos loomed defiant, and the dollah bills were pretzel bags floating on a greasy gray liquid highway. Nearby, the homeless guy the kids knew as "Fenster" farted quietly, asleep on a park bench festooned with a little plaque reading WE MISS YOU, ANDRE/9-11 NEVER FORGET/MOM AND DAD. The city gave, the city took away, and magic was for the desperate, the innocent, and the enfeebled—people at life's entrances and exits.

Waits looked at his cell phone. 3:45. His in-box showed seven unread messages, all from RESTRICTED.

Which meant Ianuzzi. Maybe the old dude had realized Waits had moved, with no forwarding address. That wouldn't please him. Someday, Waits knew, they were going to stop cutting him slack. By that time, Waits planned to be out. At first this had seemed cool, a form of social service—helping pizza-faced overachievers cope, saving them from the urge to jump into the river with a backpack full of rocks. But now he knew that was shit, and he was no Robin Hood.

"Go home, scumbag," a kick-ass beautiful girl muttered as she passed. Waits recognized her, the head of the school's Christian Club.

"Is that what Jesus would say?" he asked.

She made a face and flounced away.

"Hey, Waits, that your dad?"

Waits turned to see Cam Hong, gesturing to Fenster, the homeless guy.

"No, but he was calling out your mother's name in his sleep," Waits replied.

"You got something for me?"

"Testicles? The other half of your brain? Sorry, dude, those are your private journey."

"I'm serious, dickhead. Weed?"

Waits knew the drill with this guy. He paid half, maybe two-thirds, sold it to his football pals, and then conveniently forgot the rest. "You owe me about three hundred, Cam. You're cut off."

"How can I pay if I don't have the money?"

"Should have saved some aside. You do math, right? Supply and demand? Set the right price, keep the economy going. My people need to be fed, dude. And they won't be happy with your news."

Shit. He was repeating the same crap *they* always told him. He was becoming one of them.

"Yada yada," Cam said. "Give me one more shot. I'll come through."

"Do I hear an echo from, um, two weeks ago?" Waits said.

"This is different. A party in Westchester. Tomorrow night. It's like, Wall Street North. Like Dalton, only stupider. You know the type."

"Tell me," Waits said.

"Ghetto-wannabe, trash-talking white kids with trust funds." Cam's eyes darted to a red-haired kid wearing an NYPD cap, who was fiddling with his BlackBerry as he passed by. Cam gave Waits a conspiratorial wink. "Just like that guy."

The kid looked up. "Huh?"

"He says you're a ghetto-wannabe trash-talking trust-fund white kid," Waits said.

"I got into Olmsted on my test score," the kid said, raising an eyebrow at Cam, "and not on the ugly Asian jock quota."

"Wipe my ass, Durgin," Cam said.

"Fun for you," Byron Durgin replied, "but what's in it for me?"

"Prick."

"Wrong side of the body."

"Perve."

"That's what I like about you, Hong. The crackling wit."

"Fuck you."

"Stand in line."

"*Whoa, dudes!*" Waits held up both hands. "You've got the whole park for your marital spat. I am trying to run a business."

"Exactly," Cam said. "And you can't run a business without extending credit. It's Economics 101."

Byron burst out laughing. "Economics? Who taught you that word, Hong?" He held out his BlackBerry. "Look at this. Look at the market. Look at this line. This is my position on commodities. That red mark tells you there has been a margin call, which means I have to pay back money I don't have. Which, if you have managed to pass trigonometry and understand the first thing about stocks, tells you that I am standing here before you fucked up the butt because of the economy—and you're trying to talk economics?"

"Jesus Christ, will you two shut up?" Waits glared at Cam. "Look, dude, you owe me. I owe someone else. They extend me credit, and I extend it to you. But sooner or later, someone decides it's time to collect—and I give you three guesses who gets nailed. I have been more than nice to you. Either you're stealing from me—"

"No. Uh-uh. I don't steal," Cam interjected.

"Then you are just a shitty salesman, Cam. I would trust *him* to do a better job than you," Waits said, gesturing toward Byron.

Byron preened. "Investments I apparently suck at. But I could sell snow to an Inuit."

"Fine, I'll take him with me!" Cam piped up, grabbing Byron by the shoulder.

"What?" Byron said.

"You need quick money, right?"

"Yeah . . ." Byron said.

"And you drive?" Cam asked him.

"Well, I *have* driven," Byron said, "but just around a parking lot. . . ."

"We'll find somebody else to drive," Cam insisted. "We won't tell him what we're doing."

Byron looked confusedly at Waits, then Cam.

"Scared?" Cam said.

"Fuck no," Byron replied.

Cam put his arm around Byron and grinned. "You'll see, Waits. This will be like plucking money from a tree. You can sell these guys aspirin. They wouldn't know the difference."

Waits looked out over the river. Just beyond him, an old man held a little boy in his arms, gesturing toward the Statue of Liberty. Waits followed his arm, past the statue, where a sailboat was tacking away into the channel toward the Atlantic Ocean.

The proposition, he thought, did have some interesting potential.

"I think I can get Jimmy Capitalupo to drive," Byron said.

"Don't tell him anything," Cam said. "Tell him it's an amazing party. Tell him the babes are so horny, even he'll get laid."

"I told you I was a good salesman, not a fucking miracle worker." Byron turned to go. "Robotics. I'm out of here."

Waits watched him go, then pulled a twenty out of his pocket. "Take this. You know the Rite Aid at Wayne and Adams?"

Cam eyed him warily.

"Do you need a fucking GPS for that?" Waits said.

"What the hell am I supposed to do there?" Cam asked.

"I'd recommend the generic brand," Waits replied. "You get a bigger bang for the buck."

"Brand of *what*?"

"Aspirin," Waits said.

Cam's face fell. *"Aspirin?"*

"Your idea, Hong. For once, you had a good one."

"What am I supposed to tell Byron?"

Waits shrugged. "Up to you. But if he thinks this is all a sham, he may not have the requisite motivation."

Cam gave him a dirty look, then shoved the twenty in his pocket.

Waits watched, nursing a smile, as Cam crossed the highway.

21

JIMMY BEFORE
October 16, 8:12 P.M.

". . . So, naturally, on the topic of the death of his father, Agamnemnon, Orestes was destined to, paraphrasing Aeschylus, go postal . . ." Jimmy quickly glanced at the wall clock. Two minutes and fifteen seconds. Too slow, if he wanted to bring "The Five-Minute Oresteia" in at five minutes—and he needed this by next weekend's tournament at Regis. ". . . which left his mom, Clytemnestra, in a bit of a pickle—"

"What did you say?" blurted out Mr. Aviles, his Speech Team coach.

Jimmy groaned. He hated to break momentum. "Pickle?"

"The part about 'Naturally, on the . . .'"

"Um . . . on the topic of the death of his father, Agamnemnon, Orestes was destined to—"

"I thought so. It's *Agamemnon*."

"That's what I said!" Jimmy protested.

"You said *Agamnemnon*," Mr. Aviles said impatiently. "You put an extra *mnuh* in it."

"What?"

"An extra *N*! It's *AgaMEMnon*. Not *AgaMNEMnon*."

From the back of the room, Reina Sanchez piped up, "He's influenced by the sound of Clytemnestra."

"Exactly," Mr. Aviles agreed. "It's *ClyteMNEStra*, but *AgaMEMnon*." He rubbed his forehead. "Let's take five, kids."

As Jimmy slumped back to his seat, he saw a group of football guys perched at the door, stifling guffaws. "Mnot bad," said Ilya Vlachos.

"Although mnaybe a bit mnerdy," added Jared King.

"Will you guys leave them the fuck alone!" blasted another voice.

"Oops, it's Camn!" shrieked Ilya.

The group dispersed, laughing, as Cam Hong appeared. "Sorry," he said into the room. "They're animals."

The Speechies in the room were ignoring them, but

Jimmy felt hot under the collar. He hated the way those guys got away with that shit. Out of the corner of his eye, he could see Reina's face lighting up. How could girls—smart girls—actually think guys like that were so hot?

Jimmy ran out to the hallway, his mind rolling over possible rejoinders, witty aperçus that would cut these assholes down to size.

"Douche bags!" was the only thing that came out.

"Oh, mny!" one of them squeaked, before being hit on the head by Cam.

Jimmy slumped against the wall. Just to his right, his friend Byron Durgin was pulling something from his locker. A couple of other Speechies crowded into the doorway with him, including Reina Sanchez.

"Suffering from IQ deficit disorder," Byron muttered, nodding after the football guys.

"Why can't I think of something like that?" Jimmy muttered. "The best I can do is something like 'Douche-bags.' I always think of the perfect insult about two minutes too late."

Behind him, Reina nodded. *"L'esprit d'escalier,"* she said, grinning down the hallway toward Byron. "He taught me that."

"It's French," Byron explained. "It means the spirit of the stairs. It's like, that thing you always want to be able to say casually over your shoulder—like, bam, think of it right on the spot—as you sweep up the stairs, verbally cutting your attacker to the quick."

"How do you know that?"

"I'm a fucking genius. Didn't you hear? The one thing I can't do is drive. Which is a fucking shame, because I just got invited to a mad crazy party with panting nubile virgins in Westchester. Tomorrow night."

Reina rolled her eyes. "What will you do with panting nubile virgins, Durgin?"

"Same thing I do with you," Byron said with a grin. "Dream big."

Mr. Aviles was at the door now, ushering Reina and the team back inside. "Come on, party's over."

Jimmy lingered behind. "I can drive," he said to Byron. "Who do you know in Westchester?"

"No one. Cam invited me."

"Since when are you friends with Cam?"

"I'm a fucking genius, *and* I'm cool." Byron smiled. "He's a good guy. You saw. He just stood up for you. You know, you could reward the guy by agreeing to drive."

"To the party? No one invited me."

"I just did. Otherwise Cam and I will have to walk. Or take a train."

"I don't know. . . ." Jimmy said, turning toward the door.

"You'll get laid."

Jimmy stopped. "You think?"

Byron slammed his locker shut, flinging a forty-pound backpack over his shoulder. "Recite the Five-Minute Whooziwhat, and you will have them grabbing at your fig leaf, dude."

22

CAM AFTER
October 17, 11:42 P.M.

It hurt.

God, did it hurt.

He couldn't breathe.

These fuckers from Ignatius Hall always did this kind of shit. Piling on the Big Guy. Like they really needed to. Like they weren't going to wipe up Olmsted anyway.

It wasn't fair. All he wanted to do was play. He loved this game. He loved his teammates, the strategy, the way you could outwit someone twice your weight just by using your brain, the faces on his teammates when it all was going right. Football was fun, not a war, and *when were these goons going to learn that*?

He twisted. He pushed. Get off!

Get off!

"Cam?"

Hearing the voice, he blinked.

As the massive flank of the Ignatius fullback dissipated, Cam had the odd feeling that he had died, and he was now looking up into the face of an angel.

He didn't realize angels had wrinkles, big noses, and lipstick.

"Time out . . . ," he said.

"Doctor!" shouted the lipsticked mouth. *"Dr. Wexler, come quickly!"*

The world was reassembling—a bed, a standing IV bag, a curtain suspended from a metal rod, track lighting. He heard the *shhhhink* of sliding curtain rings. A white-coated doctor leaned over him, covering his face with a mask. "Take shallow breaths, young man. This is oxygen."

Cam slapped away the mask. "What—what—happened?" His throat felt as if it were coated with glass.

"Good . . . good," Dr. Wexler said. "You're doing very well. You were in a car accident, Cam. Do you remember any of it?"

"Ohhhh . . ." Cam tried to sit up, but his chest hurt.

The images were flooding back. *The drive . . . the ball game . . . country music . . . a shadow . . .*

"You hit a deer," the doctor continued. "A big doe. Happens a lot these days. It appears the deer came through the windshield at quite a velocity. The good news is, I don't see any broken ribs. You've had a fair amount of bruising, but nothing that will even keep you here overnight. You are one very lucky guy."

Jimmy, slamming on the brakes . . .

"It came out of nowhere. . . ." Cam said.

"Had the deer stayed on top of you, you might have been suffocated," Dr. Wexler replied. "But one of your passengers managed to pull it off."

"Capitalupo?" Cam said.

"He saved your life," the doctor said. "I'm thinking perhaps the steering wheel provided some protection, too."

"I doubt that," Cam said with a grimace. "I wasn't anywhere near it."

The doctor looked momentarily confused. "Well, we're only concerned about your health here, Cameron. Unfortunately, after you recover, the police will want to see you. Driving without a license is very serious business."

"But—I wasn't driving!" Cam protested.

Dr. Wexler checked his clipboard. "Says here the police found you in the driver's seat, Cam."

"How could that be? Jimmy was driving. He would tell you. Where is he?"

"Actually," Dr. Wexler said, stepping aside, "you can say hi to him right now."

Cam turned. Behind the doctor, looking pale and nervous, was Jimmy Capitalupo.

23

11:48 P.M.

"Jimmy?" Cam couldn't believe how happy he was to see a familiar face. "Dang, Jimmy, I can't believe this shit."

"Me neither," Jimmy mumbled. "You okay?"

"Do I *look* okay, asshole?" Cam managed a weak smile. He felt his voice cracking and turned away. "You seem all right. I'm glad. How's Byron?"

"Fine. Both of us are fine." Jimmy was sweating. His clothes were ridiculous, even for him—a plaid button-down shirt and khaki pants that seemed to belong to a fourth grader. He glanced fitfully over his shoulder at the door. Just outside, the nurse and Dr. Wexler were conferring with a cop. "Cam, I'm . . . um, really happy you survived. For a long time I thought . . ."

"You know what they told me?" Cam said. "They

said I was in the driver's seat. Incompetent bastards."

"Um, they said that?"

Cam eyed the cop. "They're not going to think I was driving, right?"

"I don't know. . . ."

"I mean, maybe the deer, like, pushed me across the seat?" Cam frowned. "Only that wouldn't make sense. You tell me. *You* were in the driver's seat."

"I—" Jimmy cast his eyes downward and let out a deep sigh. "Um, well, it wasn't the deer. It was me."

Cam didn't know whether to take this as a joke. Jimmy had a weird sense of humor. "Right."

Jimmy began pacing. "Oh, God, I'll be saying this in confession the rest of my life if I don't say it now. I did it. I dragged you over, to make it look like you were driving."

"You *what*?"

"So I wouldn't be caught driving without a license."

"I thought you had a license!"

"I lied." Jimmy finally stopped and faced Cam. His hands were shaking.

"That is one sick fucking thing to do, Jimmy!"

"Cam, it was dark, and there was this huge deer—I was panicked. I wasn't thinking straight. I thought you were dead!"

Cam sprang up on his elbow, fighting back the head pounding and chest ache. "You did it *because you thought I was dead*, you sick motherfucker? So you wouldn't get in trouble for driving?" Jimmy's eyes were tearing up, and Cam turned away in disgust. "I don't believe this. And that scumbucket Byron didn't stop you? Where the fuck is he, anyway?"

"We went to the p-p-party," Jimmy said, wiping his nose. "Afterward. We walked there. We were too scared to face the cops, so we hid in the woods—"

"You left me all alone in the car? *Left me for dead behind the steering wheel?*"

Jimmy nodded. "I'm sorry, Cam. We were scared. I was an idiot. Anyway, Byron told me I'd be thrown in jail if they caught me."

"What else did Byron tell you?" Cam pressed.

"Nothing. We were running. It was raining. We got to the party and this guy gave us dry clothes. We got separated. Then the cops came. They'd found my cell phone. I must have left it in the car. They took me away. At the station house I told them what had happened—"

"*Except the one tiny detail about you being the driver!*"

"*I will straighten that out, okay?* Give me a chance. I

told them that Byron and I ran away. I thought they were going to put me in jail—you know, leaving the scene of the accident. Then they told me you were here in the hospital—"

"Byron didn't want to come with you?"

"I don't know where he is. Maybe still at the party. The cops took only me. We could call him."

Cam rubbed his forehead. This was supposed to have been easy. He should have been heading home now, pockets full of cash—not in some dipshit hospital with a deer imprint on his chest, a wrecked car, traitorous friends, and missing envelope.

"Jimmy . . . Byron didn't *bring* anything to the party?"

Jimmy gave him a look. "What do you mean, bring anything? Like a house gift?"

"House gift? What the fuck is a *house gift*?"

"What are you talking about, Cam? We didn't go *shopping* that night!"

Cam sank back into the pillow. He felt a migraine coming on.

Jimmy didn't know. He was clueless. Byron hadn't told him anything.

Which meant Byron still had the stuff.

"Tell me, Jimmy," Cam said, "does Byron think I'm dead too?"

Jimmy shrugged. "Maybe. We both—you looked really bad, Cam. I wish we could tell him you're okay. He's probably still at the party."

Still at the party. Still selling. Keeping everything for himself.

"He must think he's the luckiest fucking guy in the world," Cam mumbled.

"What?"

Cam propped himself up on his elbows. His forehead clanged. "Let's give old Byron a little call."

"You won't reach him," Jimmy said. "His BlackBerry died."

There was a knock at the door, and Dr. Wexler came in. "Well, I have happy news. All your signs are good, Cam. Now, I just spoke with your parents, and they are very eager to see you. You can stay here overnight if you wish and they'll drive up to see you, but they've agreed to send a car for you right now if you'd like to be released."

There was a quick rap on the door, and a policeman entered, holding out a cell phone. "Here you go, doctor. We'll see you tomorrow."

"Thank you," Dr. Wexler said, pocketing the phone as the cop left. "Odd. A moment ago they were insisting on talking to you. They cornered me while I was on the phone to your parents, and your father insisted on speaking to them."

"I'll take the ride," Cam said.

Dr. Wexler smiled. "The nurse will give you a set of instructions. Precautions, mostly. We need to be careful about concussions, that sort of thing. I want you to take it easy for a few days, and I'm recommending no football—practice or games—until you see your own doctor for a follow-up. Which will be in two weeks."

"Deal," Cam said, shaking the doctor's hand.

"You're not disappointed?" Dr. Wexler asked.

"This will give me the opportunity to join the knitting club," Cam said.

The doctor gave him a wink and a thumbs-up. As his footsteps receded, Jimmy looked toward the hallway, baffled. "I can't believe they left. The cops."

"My dad talked to them. I believe he made a generous donation to the local police department. That is his modus fucking operandi, and we are leaving." Cam leaned into Jimmy. "And you're taking the trip with me, bro."

"Thanks," Jimmy said. "You can drop me off on your corner—"

"We're not going home," Cam said. "We're going to that party."

Jimmy recoiled. "Are you crazy? You're supposed to take it easy. It was a stupid party, anyway."

Cam slowly swung his legs around the side of the bed. "As soon as I do this fucking paperwork and get out of here, we are going to find Byron."

PART THREE
IT COMES TOGETHER;
IT FALLS APART

24

REINA
October 18, 12:07 A.M.

Chunk.

The metal gate made way too loud a noise as she slammed it shut. She looked around to see if anyone had noticed. Across the street a taxi honked, and she jumped. The bag was insanely heavy and dug into her shoulder.

At that moment, Reina could not imagine hating anyone more than Waits.

She glanced at his note. *Don't move till I get back.*

The balls. Who did he think he was? He expected her to just *sit* there like Penelope, waiting for her returning hero? Like she was too stupid to see the obvious. If those two yahoos weren't Mafia, they were cops—either way, they would be after the bag too. And there she would be, obedient Reina, waiting to be either mugged or arrested by a guy named Scrotum.

And this seemed totally okay to Waits.

Uh, no. He had to be taught a lesson. That son of a bitch needed to learn to take care of his own dirty laundry.

She turned away from the shop, walking quickly, weighing the possibilities. She'd already rejected the idea of just leaving the bag in the locked shop. That would be inviting a break-in, and Ted would blame her. Spending the cash was a sweet possibility—Waits couldn't exactly report her to the police for that—but if the bills were stolen, they might be marked. And if they were, she would be too.

So she was stuck.

For now.

She looked both ways, then slid off to the left. First things first. She had to get to Blowback. On the way, there would be a hiding place, somewhere that she could leave the bag. She'd text him—make it a little hard for him, maybe make him have to play a game or solve a riddle.

She looked nervously over her shoulder. Mr. Saltonstall, the old dude who sat on the second-floor tenement balcony, gave her a desultory wave.

Reina ducked around the corner, onto Capulet Street.

Someone was blasting Chuck Berry from behind an open tenement window, and someone else was cooking a dish that smelled of garlic and ginger. From across the way a voice moaned, and a rodent skittered across the alley. She felt the hairs on her legs and arms stand up. Shifting the bag from her right to her left shoulder, she ran to the end of the block.

There, open to the night like a tyrannosaur jaw, was a huge industrial Dumpster. She stopped. It was perfect. Waits would call her eventually, and she would give him the location. Finding it would be a bit of a messy operation—but Waits deserved nothing less. He might even have to negotiate with a supersize rat or two. Actually, it was kind of fun to imagine.

She unhooked the bag and drew her arm back.

A voice, just around the next corner, made her freeze.

"Whadya go and order that shit for—latte, shmatte—what are you, a faggot or something?"

An answer shot back: "It's the twenty-first century, Gramps. They don't serve castor oil in these places."

"We was supposed to *tail* him, that's all—wait for him to make his drop, then take him in. But no. You want to be a fucking hero and do a *sting* operation—like he's gonna think *we're* the drop and just give us the money. Well, guess what? Mob guys don't order faggot coffee. He knew! He knew right away!"

Into the light walked the two guys who had met Waits at Smitty's. They were arguing intently, gesturing at each other.

Reina backed away, clutching the shoulder bag. The sound of it landing in the Dumpster would draw their attention.

She glanced left and right. Across the street, at the opposite end of the block, people streamed out of the subway stop for the D train. If she kept to the building shadow and walked fast, away from the two men, they wouldn't notice.

"It had to be there, I tell you," the old man was shouting. "It had to!"

"Well, it ain't there now."

"How the fuck do you know?"

"Because you and I have been walking away, arguing like old ladies for the last five minutes."

Reina picked up the pace, stumbling on a crack in the sidewalk. She raced into the street, eyes on the subway entrance.

HONNNKK!

She jumped back, barely avoiding a car that was

barreling down the street at breakneck speed.

A black Hummer.

Figured. People who drove those monsters thought they owned the world.

Looking both ways, she crossed the street, plunged into the emerging subway crowd, and disappeared down the stairs.

25

12:19 A.M.

"Hey, Gino? It's Reina."

Reina pressed her ear to the cell phone as the train emerged from underground. For what felt like the thousandth time, she glanced over her shoulder toward the back of the train car, guarding against anything suspicious. Fortunately this crowd was more hipster than gangster.

"Yo, 'sup, cuz?" crackled her cousin Gino's voice from the other end, barely audible above the thumping din of the music in the club. "You got tired of the SATs?"

Reina fought back the words that were on the tip of her tongue.

Help me, Gino, I've got a bag full of hot money and I'm scared and all I wanted to do was have some fun tonight. . . .

Not here. Not with other people in earshot. She realized she should have texted him, but the sound of his voice was worth the call. Gino was so upbeat and reassuring.

"I—I, uh, just want to make sure I'm on the list tonight?" she said.

"Well, I will consult my staff and get back to you on that issue." Gino cackled. "Uh, ye-ah. *Of course you are!* The boys know you. You coming alone?"

"Yes." Reina caught herself. *Byron. You got that hysterical call from Byron. He's meeting you.* "I mean, no. Also Byron Durgin? And he's bringing someone, I think."

"Cool. I'll put 'em on the list."

"Thanks, G."

She closed the phone and took a deep breath. Gino had seen everything. Gino would know what to do. She would deal with the bag when she got there—hide it in another Dumpster, maybe. Force Waits to come looking for it.

As the train sped across the bridge, she gazed out over the blazing Manhattan skyline. During the day it was a force of human energy, exclamation points in steel and marble, but at night it was all about stories—each window a tiny movie screen that turned and danced with the train's approach. When she was little, she and her dad would list all the things they imagined people were doing behind each window: dipping stale chicken nuggets in milk, breaking up with someone by e-mail and sending it to the wrong address, hearing the Rolling Stones for the first time, discovering a dead pet goldfish, peeling a mango. *Odds are, every one of those things is DEFINITELY occurring,* her dad always said.

For the first time all night, she smiled.

Soon she'd be dancing away her fears . . . maybe even laughing about what had just happened . . . imitating Scrotum . . . figuring out why Byron had sounded so horrible over the phone . . .

He had sounded truly frantic, nearly incoherent. Dear, sad, brilliant Byron. So smart, so uncomfortable with himself. She never could understand him—but he was the kind of guy who staked his personality on the ability to lament that no one understood him. If he ever got to Blowback, she'd be playing Patient Listener all night.

Inscrutable.

As the train sped across the bridge, she instinctively clutched Waits's bag. She was beginning to smell like his aftershave, which was really annoying her.

Her cell phone vibrated, and she glanced at the screen: UNAVAILABLE NUMBER.

"Hello?" she said tentatively.

"Where are you?"

Waits.

If there was one thing Reina hated, it was cell phone callers who blocked their numbers—and *still* expected you to know who they were by the sound of their voices.

Presumptuous.

"It depends," she said.

"I've been trying to call you!"

"Have you? Well. Maybe you could start by telling me who you are."

"This is Waits! You were supposed to stay at Smitty's."

"Oh, darn. Guess I forgot."

"Christ, Reina, I hope you aren't carrying that shoulder bag."

"What if I am?"

"Damn it! Where can I meet you?"

"Who says I want to meet you? Maybe I'll keep all the money. Maybe I've spent it already."

"*You opened it?* That was not a good idea, Reina. If you have that bag, you are in deep shit. Trust me. *Where are you?*"

Reina glanced out the window. The train was descending toward the tunnel on the Manhattan side. "I'm on the Williamsburg Bridge. But not for long, so we'll lose contact. I'll be at Blowback. My cousin's friend owns it. It's a club. But it's very hard to get in unless you're on the list. Or you're a celebrity."

"I know what it is. Reina, listen to me. Whatever you do, don't go in there with that bag. You know the Acropolis Diner, on Tenth Avenue? Meet me there."

"Um, *you* are not the one calling the shots, I think. And I am not playing your stupid game anymore. I thought you'd like to know that."

"It's not a game. It is *so* not a game. Look, if you order something I'll pay, if you're worried about that—"

"No problem, I've got cash."

"Reina, please, just go to the diner. Don't say another word about money over this phone. Make sure you are not being followed—especially by those two goons who were at Smitty's. I'm in a cab now. I will try to get there before you."

"For your information, I saw those guys," Reina said, "back in Brooklyn. They are nowhere near me, Waits. So I'm heading for Blowback. If you're not there, I'll leave the bag behind the bar. Or maybe I'll toss it in the river."

"Reina, don't do that! Whatever you do, don't—"

"What? What? Oops, my phone's going dead." She hung up. Almost immediately the phone rang again, but she let it go to voice mail.

As the train plunged toward street level on the Lower East Side, a ragged-looking man with sharp eyes stumbled toward her, paused, and sat down next to her shoulder bag. "Got something for me?" he said.

Her heart began to race. She fingered her phone. Could she text for help without looking at the keypad, before service really went out?

"Um . . . ," she said, sliding to her left as far as she could Above her was the emergency brake. She could pull that, and the train would stop. She could scream bloody murder. Someone in the car would jump to her defense.

The guy leaned closer, whispering. "Are you the Secretary of State?"

"What?" Reina said.

"Are you the Secretary of the Interior?" he asked.

"No!" Reina replied.

"Do you have a cigarette? Or a bagel?"

"Sorry."

Reina got up and moved to the other end of the car. She could feel all eyes conspicuously not following her. As she sat back down, the guy was slumping onto the spot she'd vacated, falling asleep.

Calm down. You are being paranoid.

If anyone was in trouble, it was Waits. If someone was after that money, they'd be following him, not her.

And she would be surrounded by Cousin Gino and his entire entourage of ex-football players and Christopher Street muscle boys.

Quickly, while she still had coverage, she redialed her last number.

"Reina Leina Bing-Bang!" Gino shouted. "'Sup, girl?"

"Can you put one more name on? Waits?"

"Waits? Like Tom Waits?"

"I don't know his first name."

"Done."

"Tha—"

The phone died. The subway windows rattled as the train entered the tunnel.

Waits would follow her to the club. She would call the shots from there.

26

WAITS

"I got it," Waits said into the phone, shutting the taxi window to block the wind noise. "I got the money."

The cab flew onto the Brooklyn Bridge. Overhead the threaded cables shrouded the cityscape like spiderwebs. So far, no traffic. He had told the driver to hit the FDR South, until it curved around the bottom of the city and became the West Side Highway North. With luck he'd be at Blowback by 12:35 or 12:40.

The voice at the other end, as always, was slow to answer, a pregnant silence that seemed to say *I am giving you time to correct this absolutely stupid-as-shit thing you just said.* "Youse got it. . . ." the voice finally replied, growly and deep. "Kid tells me he's got it. He doesn't show at the drop, makes my guys look like fuckin' baboons, and he expects me to believe he's got it."

"I was followed to Smitty's," Waits replied. "So I left. And then they closed early. Sorry, Sal, but we have to change the location of the drop."

"So . . . what is supposed to mean this 'got it'? As in, 'got it in my hands right now'?"

"As in, I will put the money in your fucking hands if you meet me at Blowback right now, Sal," Waits said. "It's on the corner of West and—"

"I know where the fucking place is," Ianuzzi said. "You think I don't know shit about the clubs? My conundrum is this: I am supposed to interrupt my night, my precious personal time, to follow *your* orders?"

He let out a snapping, sibilant hiss, a snarl masquerading as a laugh.

"Sal, all I'm saying is if you happen to be in the city, that's where I'll be tonight," Waits said. "With the cash. If you'd rather, I can give it to you another day. You're in control, dude."

That would do it, Waits thought. The guy wanted the money, and he would show.

"I am, as a matter of fact, finishing up a nice baba au rhum at Umberto's," Ianuzzi said, with a lusty belch. "But

I will sacrifice my usual postprandial nap in order to have my guy take me to pay you a special visit. I trust you realize what a rare occasion this is. So you better have the fucking cash."

Waits swallowed. He felt his insides shrinking. "I will, Sal."

"And Watts?"

"Yes, Sal?"

"It's Mr. Ianuzzi to you."

Waits swallowed hard. The last words he heard before the line went dead were *Feets, get the fuckin' car, pronto.*

27

REINA
October 18, 12:27 A.M.

"Hey, girl, 'sup?" said Tito the bouncer, with a massive grin spreading across his massive face.

Reina clutched the shoulder bag tight, trying to look normal as she rushed past him. "'Sup, Tito," she said. "Did you see Waits?"

Tito scowled. "Don't you be telling me you're hanging with that hunk of doody."

"He . . . left something. At Smitty's? I brought it for him. I mean . . . he was a customer."

"Girl, you are looking tight as a drum. You need to take my Pilates class—"

"Right. Okay. See you!"

She slipped inside and felt herself being sucked in by

a swarm of dancing, laughing people. Usually this made her feel euphoric and free. Tonight, all she could feel was the weight of the bag.

Her eyes darted left and right as she made her way across the dance floor. It wouldn't be long before Waits got here. Out of the corner of her eye, she spotted Gino chatting up a dark-haired girl with cleavage and legs and not much in between. No getting his attention now.

"Hey, babe, would you like to check that?" a grinning guy called out to her—Brad, Brandon, Brent, Ben—they all had names like that. He was gesturing to a coat room by the door.

"Yes!" Reina said, quickly unhooking the bag.

She handed it to him and then plunged into the crowd, not bothering to take her ticket.

28

BYRON
October 18, 12:28 A.M.

"Coooool!" MC squealed as the car approached Blowback.

Byron's fingers shook. He had been cut off, tailgated, honked at, cursed at, middle-fingered, and brights-flashed from the moment he hit the West Side Highway. The experience of driving in New York City was a thousand times more awful than he had ever imagined.

Doing it in the company of MC Reemer was sheer insanity.

Her CD mix, which she had played through twice, sounded like outtakes from *Siberia's Got Talent*. She rode with her window open, randomly screaming ejaculations of inappropriate exuberance such as "I love yoooou, Big Apple!" She wore a short, flower-patterned dress that spoke Wal-Mart 2006 Yellow Tag Summer Clearance Sale rack. Her short hair was gelled to within an inch of its life, and when she wasn't screaming, she was bouncing in her seat and applying makeup in the visor mirror.

Byron could not believe this girl. Human beings of this age group did not behave in this way. He knew North Dakota was not New York, but it wasn't the Oort cloud either.

It didn't help that she'd dressed him in her dad's sturdy solid-color Aramark "dresswear" that made him look like an insurance salesman on Casual Friday.

"Woooo-*HOOOOOO!*" MC shrieked as Byron steered carefully down West Street past the club, around a small throng of bridge-and-tunnel types waiting to get in.

"You are embarrassing me," Byron said through gritted teeth.

She grinned. "Do you know what a big deal this is for someone like me?"

"That's right. I forgot. Being raised by wolves in the wilderness and all . . ." Making a left turn into a side street, he headed for a space being vacated by an SUV with Jersey plates.

"I can't believe this—Blowback, just like I pictured it!" MC said, face plastered to the window. "You actually *know* the person who owns this club?"

"I know the cousin of someone who runs the club," Byron said. "I think she said she put our names on a list. Now can you please shut up so I can concentrate on parking?"

After six tries he gave up and double-parked next to a battered Corolla. The fact that MC was laughing at him the whole time did not help. "That was the worst parallel parking job I ever saw," she said.

"Thanks for the support," Byron replied. "Why didn't *you* drive?"

"That wouldn't be nearly as much fun." She leaned over and planted a kiss on his cheek. "You are so adorable when you get frustrated. Especially when you're wearing my dad's clothes."

"Now *that's* sick." Byron felt a cough coming on. He went to turn off the heat but it wasn't on. This entire night had been one long tumble down the rabbit hole, and he realized he'd not reached bottom.

"How do I look?" She was smiling at him. She had that annoying, expectant gaze that said *Anything you do will live up to the cuddlicious stereotype into which I have just placed you.*

The thing was, as much as he hated to admit it, as much as he would never dare to say it to her, as much as he suspected his creeping cold/flu/sniffle/whatever-it-was was affecting his brain and he *never until this second* would have entertained this thought, against all odds a new fact had leaped out of the primordial ooze of his misery:

She did something for him.

God damn it.

"Well. Um," he stammered. "Your makeup . . . ?"

Her smile vanished. "What?"

"Well, it's . . ." Byron pulled down her sun visor again, which had a convenient light of its own. "It's great. I mean, the colors. But maybe you can, I don't know, wipe off a little around the eyes?"

"It's too much?" MC said, taking out a makeup sponge.

"And maybe the rest of the face. You don't really need it. I mean, you look pretty good without it."

"Seriously?"

"I mean, the lipstick is nice." *Oh, dear God, I did not say that.* Byron grabbed the door handle. "We really have to go."

"Just a sec."

He got out of the car and waited, tapping his roof with his fingers, tapping the cobblestoned road with his feet. A gang of kids was walking down the street, all paired off in gay and straight couples, laughing at some comment and looking like they'd known each other their whole lives. Across the street a guy and a girl were leaning against a brick wall, just stroking each other's hair and saying nothing. Smiling.

Then the sidewalk began to shake.

He heard a car roaring around the corner, its woofers blasting a Frank Sinatra track.

Byron turned to see a black Hummer speed up the street, just as MC pushed open the Town Car's passenger door.

"Be careful!" Byron shouted.

EEEEEEEEEEE . . . The Hummer's tires screeched against the cobblestones as it swerved. "Asshole!" yelled someone from inside.

"Fucking maniac!" MC screamed, picking up a beer bottle from the street and tossing it at the car.

With a loud *thock*, it made contact with the Hummer's rear door. The car came to a sudden stop and began accelerating backward. The back window rolled down, revealing a stone-faced older guy with a killer tan, pockmarked cheeks, and mirror sunglasses.

"Oh, Jesus . . . ," Byron said, grabbing MC's arm. *"Come on!"*

"Did you see what that guy did?" MC said, struggling to pull loose. "We can't let him get away with that!"

"Yes, we can," Byron said, plunging into the crowd.

"He called me an asshole!"

"You are, by local standards. This is New York. *Which* wormhole did you say you were from?"

MC stopped short, nearly making him fall to the ground. "That wasn't a very nice thing to say."

"That was a stupid thing to do!"

"You just haven't been very nice to me all night."

"You haven't exactly been easy to deal with!"

"Oh?" Her eyes were huge, her fists firmly on hips. "Give me an example of how. How have I been anything but cheerful and fun and friendly?"

Byron exhaled. "Dear God, give me a break. . . ."

"An example, Byron. Go ahead. Just one!"

"Okay. Okay. You laugh at me. You treat me like I'm your chauffeur—"

"That's two. And for your information, I laugh *with* you. And I was giving you *space*, to help you learn to drive."

"Fine. You're right. I suck. Are we done now?"

MC cocked her head, looking at him as if he were a mildly lagged third grader who'd forgotten his homework.

"Um, *which* one of us was raised in the wilderness? The next step, Byron, is usually an apology."

"Wait. *Me* apologize?"

"Say you're sorry, or I go home. With the you-know-what."

"But—you have this totally backward—" He took a deep breath and counted to ten. People were starting to stare, and she wasn't budging. This was quickly turning lose-lose. "Okay, I'm sorry. I'm sorry! Okay?"

MC gave him a dreamy smile. "Now kiss me."

"*What?*"

"Come on," she said teasingly. "Am I that disgusting to you? You told me you were straight! You liar!"

A girl in line let out a sarcastic laugh. "I been there, honey."

"Sister!" MC slapped her five.

"Just a minute! I *am* straight, and you are not disgusting, all right?" Byron said.

"Is that the best you can do?" chimed the girl in line. "Tell her she's *hot*, baby, 'cause she is."

Byron nodded. "Right. I mean, without all the makeup and all. Yeah. That's right."

"Really?" MC said, brightening. "You think?"

Byron nodded, feeling like his body thermostat had

just activated the sprinkler system. "Yes. Sort of. I mean, yes. But—but—oh God, you are *so* not getting what's happening here."

"Oh Byron, of course I get it!" MC pulled him away from the line. With her back to the crowd, she pulled the envelope from inside her bra and dangled it in front of him. "We have an adventure ahead of us. And all the little pillies are still here. Well, okay, most of them . . ."

"*Most* of them?" Byron's heart was sinking. "How many did you take?"

"Enough to feel *fabulous*!" She spun around, holding the envelope high and releasing it into the air.

Byron dived after it, snatching it just before it landed in a potted plant.

"Oops," MC said with a giggle.

Byron peered inside the envelope, trying to judge how many pills were missing. "Are you okay? I mean, you didn't do anything dumb, right?"

"See, you *do* care. . . ." MC smiled. "Just one. Or maybe two. I'm really vibing, Byron."

"I have an idea," Byron said, heading for the door. "You stay here and continue to vibe. I'll see you in an hour."

"There you go again!" MC ran around in front of him. "You are so inconsistent! I cannot understand you."

"This is not about you, MC!"

"You're right, it's about both of us." With a sudden lunge, MC took the envelope from his hand. "Fifty-fifty. I am not leaving your side."

"Fine." Byron plowed forward. He could not wait for this night to be over.

29

JIMMY
October 18, 12:29 A.M.

"I'm good," Cam insisted to the nurse who was trying to keep him on his bed.

"I know, dear," the nurse insisted, "but you can't just up and leave without filling out the paperwork."

"So give it to me!" Cam said.

"It's being prepared right now."

Beep.

Beep.

Beep.

Jimmy didn't know which was more obnoxious, the argument or the constant chirping of Cam's cell phone. Fishing it out of the hospital duffel, he expected to see a message from Cam's mom. She had been calling the hospital every five minutes.

This definitely wasn't Mrs. Hong.

im screwed—w

"Uh, Cam . . . ?" Jimmy said as the nurse stormed off. "Who's 'w'?"

"An ex-President of the United States," Cam mumbled.

At that moment another nurse came into the room with an empty wheelchair and a stack of papers. *"Voilà!"* she said. "Fill these out, then you can get dressed and you're free to go home to your mom and dad."

Cam was staring at the wheelchair. "I don't need *that*."

"You do, sweetheart, if you want to be discharged," the nurse replied. "Hospital rules."

BEEP.

Jimmy glanced at the cell screen while Cam swung his legs around the bed. It was another message:

in traffic. heading to blowback. need the $ NOW or ur fucked—w

"Um, Cam . . . ?"

Cam was arguing with the nurse, insisting he could walk on his own, limping around the bed like an old man.

Jimmy raised his voice. "Cam, you have two text messages. They look important."

"If it's the Olympic Committee, tell them I'll be at training tonight," Cam shot back.

The nurse smiled. "A spirited young fellow, isn't he?"

As she left, Jimmy pulled Cam closer. "Will you please read this?"

Cam glanced impatiently at the screen and suddenly went still. "Shit."

"Who is it?" Jimmy asked.

"Jimmy, do you have access to a cash machine?"

"Well, yeah. I have high-school checking . . ."

"I need some cash."

"Now?" Jimmy couldn't believe this. "What is this all about?"

"Just a few hundred, Jimmy. Can I trust you? Can I count on you? Are you my friend?"

"Well, yeah, but—"

"Thanks, dude!" Cam barged out of the room and into the hallway in his hospital gown, calling over his shoulder, "We're not going to that party after all. You and I are heading into the city—to Blowback!"

"Mr. Hong?" the nurse called out. *"Mr. Hong, you need to change into your clothes first!"*

30

WAITS
October 18, 12:48 A.M.

Where was she?

Where the fuck was she?

Waits charged through the club. The cab had hit bad traffic near Battery Park City. A fender bender. Bumper-to-bumper for ten fucking minutes.

His heart's pounding created a cross beat with the music. It dislocated him, making him aggravated and light-headed at the same time. He didn't care who he was pushing around. No one seemed to notice anyway.

He hated the fact that he had to be here.

He had been so close. *So close.*

All he'd needed to do was make the drop. He'd handled the two chumps perfectly at Smitty's—not that it took a Ph.D. to recognize they were cops. He'd called their game, psyched them out. All he'd had to do was walk around the block slowly, return, and get the bag. If the real drop showed, great. If not, he could work out another drop with Ianuzzi over the phone. No big deal.

He'd be done by now. On his way out of the racket. Requesting college admissions packets from Middlebury and Kenyon on his new Mac.

So fucking close.

There.

He stopped short, nearly knocking over a willowy, half-lidded blonde whose lips tried desperately to form words as she fell into the arms of three friends.

Reina was at the bar, downing a drink and looking around nervously. As he made his way over, she looked his way and winced.

"Hey," he said.

Her features tightened and she said nothing.

"Look, I'm sorry," he continued. "I know I probably sounded like an asshole over the phone. It's just . . . somebody's after me."

Reina nodded. "I can see why."

"This is the last time, you know."

"That's nice."

"For . . . this business." He took a deep breath. She wasn't going to give an inch. "So. Where is it?"

"I don't know, exactly."

"What do you mean, *you don't know exactly*?" Waits suddenly felt swelteringly hot. "You told me you would bring it here."

"I did." Reina shrugged.

Keep a lid on, he told himself. "Look, Reina, I know you're angry at me for leaving you with . . . you know. But we can't keep playing Twenty Questions here—"

Reina spun on him. The fury in her eyes was almost a solid, palpable thing. "I said I brought it. I brought a coat too. But when you want to dance and relax and have a good time—when you want to be in a club like a normal person—you don't keep all your stuff with you."

Waits began backing away. "Okay. Thanks. I owe you, Reina."

"Keep the change."

He spun around and began heading for the coat room. But wending its way slowly across the dance floor, like an old barge, was a shock of salt-and-pepper hair among an undulating sea of colors.

Feets.

Waits ducked. Keeping his head low, he took a longer

route to the coatroom and barged into an employee entrance door. "Can I help you?" a bored but incredibly hot Latino chick asked.

"I'll get it myself," Waits said.

The room was cavernous, racks and racks of coats, with shoulder bags piled everywhere he looked.

Fucking Reina.

This was going to take a long, long time.

31

BYRON
October 18, 12:48 A.M.

Elbowing his way back through the crowd toward the front door of Blowback, Byron thought he saw Cam at least four times.

Each sighting was like a punch to the gut. He hadn't realized how many people looked like Cam. Maybe it was psychological. Cam used to come here. He'd bragged about it.

If Cam were really a regular, Byron realized, then maybe some of these people were Cam's friends. Maybe they were hoping to see him.

He felt shrouded in guilt, like he should be wearing a sandwich board with the message HERE WALKS THE SHIT-HEAD RESPONSIBLE FOR THE DEATH OF CAM HONG. HE

ARRANGED THE TRANSPORTATION, HE GOT AN INCOM-
PETENT TO DRIVE, AND AFTER THE ACCIDENT HE LEFT
THE SCENE!

But instead he just grunted, "Excuse me," as he barged forward. He only stopped when he'd reached a knot of people just before the door, arguing with the bouncer.

MC squeezed up next to him. "That was fun."

"Your bar is set too low," Byron replied. "Who *are* these people?"

MC gave him a bemused look. "Byron? Are you always like this?"

"Like what?"

"Agitated. Nervous. Is it me? Am I doing this to you?"

"No!"

"Then is it the . . . you-know-whats? 'Cause we don't have to do what we came here to do, it if you really don't want to. I mean, I just thought this would be an adventure."

"You drive a hard bargain for an adventurer."

MC shrugged. "The fifty-fifty? I was just trying to be fair. I'm not into people taking advantage of me. But I don't mean to railroad. We could renegotiate if you want."

"No, no, it's all right." The argument with the bouncer was turning ugly, and Byron rubbed his forehead.

He felt MC's hand closing over his. He started to pull

away, but for some the reason the effort just petered out. "We could also go somewhere else and forget the whole thing," she said.

"Look," Byron said, "um, let's just do this. We split the proceeds, pay off Waits, return the car, and find out what happened to Jimmy."

"And then—?" MC asked.

The arguing group was now being led away by two guys who looked like they'd subsisted on T-bone steak since birth. The remaining bouncer, not looking too cheery, glared at Byron and MC. "End of the line, kids."

"Byron Durgin?" Byron said, gesturing toward a hand-written list on a makeshift podium. "I should be there? Reina Sanchez was supposed to—"

Glancing briefly at the list, the bouncer wordlessly pulled aside the silk rope and gestured for Byron to enter.

MC squealed, throwing her arms around Byron and kissing his ear from behind, so loudly that his eardrum popped.

"Ow—don't *ever* do that again," Byron said as they walked in.

"Who do you know here?" MC asked, dropping her voice to a conspiratorial whisper. "Do you know, like, everybody? Who should we start with? What's our opening line? Is there some kind of, like, body language we should use—?"

"*I don't know! I've never done this before!*" Byron snapped. "We have to be quiet. Don't forget, what we're doing happens to be *illegal*."

"Right." MC straightened her dress out. "Right. I know. I am feeling like so Jennifer Garner at this moment."

Byron grabbed her by the arms. "This is serious, MC. We owe somebody a lot of money. This guy, Waits? Trust me, he is a motherfucker. From what I know, he has ties to the Mob. Close ones. So we have to be discreet and fast. Got it?"

"Check. So what do we do?"

"Let's dance. I'll look around and see what other people are doing."

"Like, other drug dealers?" MC whispered. "Do we have to worry about, like, a turf war? I'm not packing anything—"

"Stop it!" Byron hissed. He started moving to the beat. "Oh. One other thing. If we see Reina, we should talk to her. Thank her for getting us in."

MC was giggling. "You don't dance much, do you?"

"What? I mean, yeah. No. Am I doing something wrong?"

"You're trying too hard. Just relax into the beat. Like this."

Byron watched as she spun away. She was a great dancer. Subtle and sure. "I hate you," he said.

She swooped back toward him, wrapping her arms around his shoulder and leaning in close. "Just pick up the vibe. You can do that."

Byron tried to feel the rhythm. He smiled. "Do you take lessons, or is that natural?"

"That is such a dorky question," MC said, raising her hands high over her head.

Byron imitated her motions as they traveled around the dance floor until her shoulders shook from laughing and she had to stop. "Ow, ow, ow," she said, doubled over, "I have to go to the bathroom before I wet my pants."

She pushed her way across the dance floor. As Byron watched her go, he spun around all by himself, taking in the scene: a woman naked from the waist up who was really a man, a guy in a G-string with a snake wrapped around his neck, someone of indeterminate sex with a five-foot-high purple wig and a sequined gown, bunches of people who looked like Tom Cruise and Ashton Kutcher, about a hundred girls who were too skinny to be anything but models or Olsen twins, and a bar manned by a team of buff bartenders in black tank tops. Incongruously, a big middle-aged dude with slicked-back graying hair, all dressed in black, was walking around aggressively as if suddenly teleported from the Hustler Club.

The sight of bottles against the bar's wall made Byron realize he hadn't had a thing to drink since the party in Westchester. He elbowed his way closer.

"What'll you have?" a bartender called out.

"Diet Coke—two?" Byron shouted back.

As he reached the bar, Byron could see Reina at the other end, deep in conversation with a guy.

He called out her name, but she couldn't hear him above the noise, so he began nudging through the crowd. "Yo! Reina!"

She looked very serious, angry even. Throwing up her arms, she stormed away.

And Byron could see who she'd been talking to.

Waits.

32

1:04 A.M.

Shit.

Byron burst out the front door and ran to the end of the block. There, he put his hand to his chest.

It was statistically impossible for fright to cause a heart attack in a seventeen-year-old. Wasn't it?

It was one of the many, many questions to which he did not know the answer at that moment. Like what would happen if you promised to deliver drug money and then didn't. In the movies they could shoot you for that. Or drop you in the river with cement shoes.

Stop. Breathe. Think.

Okay, this was simpler than it seemed. It was about buying and selling. Like chocolate chip cookies or lemonade. Only illegal. He would have to make enough to pay

Waits, that was all. Whatever "enough" was. Cam wasn't around to provide him with that info.

Sell, baby, sell.

He eyed a group of high school kids up the street to his left. He didn't know them, which was a good thing. One of them, a tall Latino guy with glasses, had noticed Byron's glance and nodded to him tentatively.

"Uh, hi," Byron said. "Do you guys, uh, you know, need . . . ?" His voice trailed off and he made a suggestive head gesture that he hoped would convey the desire to make a deal regarding substances.

"Need?" the guy repeated.

". . . something?" Byron quickly added, looking nervously over his shoulder. "I mean, all of you? Any of you? We could, like, go somewhere. . . ."

"Oh, my God, ew, is this like some sex thing?" piped up a black-haired girl in the group. "I am not into cluster-fucks *at all.*"

"No! I didn't—I—" Byron stammered, but the kids were walking quickly up the block away from him.

He turned back toward the club and came face-to-face with a skinny, bearded guy with droopy eyes and multiple piercings leaning against a brick wall.

"What do you got?" the guy rasped.

Byron reached into his pocket. "Pills?"

"And what *kind* of pills would these be?" the guy drawled.

Nothing.

He had no pills. He had given them to MC.

"Um . . . never mind," Byron squeaked.

"I have some weed," the guy said. "Trade? I'll show you mine if you show me yours. . . ."

Byron gulped. "Uh, I think my friends are calling. . . ."

He ran up the block, losing himself among the milling crowd. Squatting against the metal grating of a closed-up bodega, he caught his breath.

His phone rang in his pocket and he snapped it open. "Yeah?"

"Where are you?" came MC's voice.

"Outside. I saw Waits."

"Oh great, so you chickened out? I have to do this alone?"

"Just give me a minute to think this through."

"It's not fun to do this all alone! How do I start?"

"*Fun?*" The memories of the night cascaded through his mind, and he suddenly had no patience for his new partner. "This isn't *fun*, MC. Someone died for those stupid fucking pills."

"Aren't we dramatic?"

"His name was Cam, MC. Short for Cameron. And you are holding his life in your fucking hands!"

"Byron? Are you okay?"

Up the block, Byron heard the rumble of a truck. Red and white light flashed on the sidewalk.

Cops.

"Later," he said, snapping the phone shut.

Two kids were running up the street, clambering into a double-parked car. Byron squinted at the flashing vehicle. It was a tow truck, pulling just in front of a double-parked behemoth of a car—the black Hummer, showing a nasty scratch on the trunk from MC's bottle toss.

The rear window rolled down, revealing the tanned, stony face. From out of the club ran the black-clad middle-aged guy Byron had seen a moment ago, bellowing profanities at the tow truck operator.

Byron leaped to his feet, glancing up the street to the double-parked Lincoln Town Car. Fumbling for his keys, he ran over to it and jumped in. His phone was vibrating but he ignored it. He jammed the key in the ignition, looking around for a place to move it. The street was packed on both sides, and a garage just ahead said NO VACANCY.

He pulled into the street and drove slowly, stopping at

a red light on Washington Street. In his rearview mirror, he saw a tall guy wearing thin glasses and a long black coat running toward him, hand-in-hand with a willowy Asian girl who was laughing out of control, her head canted upward.

Byron figured they were running to rescue their car too. Then he heard his rear door open. "Penn Station?" the guy said.

"This isn't a cab!" Byron said.

But the girl, giggling, was climbing into the back, holding her arms to the guy, who jumped on top of her. "Shut the *door*, André!" she squealed.

Byron turned. "Uh, excuse me? This isn't a—"

HONNK!

The entire street was blowing horns at him. The guy slammed the car door shut and wrapped the girl in his arms.

HONNK! HONNNNNNK!

Byron stepped on the accelerator. The car lurched forward, patching out as he turned the corner.

"Oooh," the girl cried out. "That felt *nice*."

In the rearview mirror he saw something black and lacy flying through the air. A bare shoulder. A grunt.

"Listen, guys . . . ," Byron said, angling toward the curb. "This is, like, a private car? So I'll just pull over and . . ."

A graceful hand with long nails, painted a robin's-egg-blue pattern, reached over the seat of the car. It dropped a fifty-dollar bill onto the front seat. "Keep the change," the girl's voice said.

Byron gulped. "Okay, Penn Station," he said.

That was uptown. In the distance the Empire State Building was winking at him through the gaps between buildings. Penn Station was near that. If he kept going straight, he'd be in the vicinity. He edged back into the flow of traffic and worked up to forty miles an hour. Washington Street was a sea of green lights.

The sounds of the streets filtered in through the window, mixing with the laughter and unbucklings from behind him.

"So, you guys . . . need anything? Pills?" he asked. "I can, um, go back to the club. To my source. It'll only be a second."

"Fuck that," the guy's voice replied. "You got condoms?"

Byron laughed. But no one laughed back.

They were serious.

They'd already passed a few Duane Reades, Rite Aids, and CVSes, but there were a couple more on the next block. Byron pulled into a metered spot and grabbed the fifty off the seat. "Stay right there."

He ran into the drugstore and headed straight for the pharmacy. A petite blonde in thick glasses looked up at him impassively.

"Uh, hi," Byron said, swallowing hard to force saliva down his suddenly arid throat. "Condoms?"

"Which brand?" she asked, smiling as she leaned on the counter.

"Which brand is, like, the most popular?" Byron asked. "Like, for people who . . . *know* condoms?"

The pharmacist suddenly reached forward at waist level. Byron jumped aside, muffling a scream.

She was lying over the counter now, and Byron realized she was examining an array that had been right in front of him, condoms in different sizes, styles, and flavors. She pulled out two boxes and stood, holding them out to him with a raised eyebrow. "What did you think I was going to do, measure you?" she asked. "These two are our, um, biggest sellers."

Byron smiled wanly, putting the fifty on the counter. "Sorry. Um, both, I guess. To be on the safe side. Brand-wise."

When she handed back the change, he bolted.

He scrambled into the car. The two boxes were different brands, but the couple seemed to be in advanced stages of need, so he ripped open the first, extracted a condom, and handed it over the seat. "I'm not looking," he said helpfully.

"Aw, shit, don't you have Fourex?" the guy protested.

Byron panicked momentarily—until he saw the brand name on the other box.

God bless Duane Reade and its superior employees.

Byron opened the box and tossed back the requested item. "At your service."

33

REINA
October 18, 1:09 A.M.

"Yo, cuz—where you been?"

Reina felt a bearlike grip take her from behind and lift her high off the ground. She let out an involuntary scream.

"Whoa, whoa, whoa, it's just me." Gino set her down and turned around, a big smile quickly fading from his face. "Hey, are you okay, Reina-Beina?"

Reina nodded. She didn't realize she'd been crying, but her hand was lifting upward to wipe her cheeks dry. "Just . . . an argument."

"So whose kneecaps am I breaking?" Gino said with mock toughness, scanning the room.

Reina smiled. "I think I did it already. Metaphorically speaking."

"Here in Blowback no metaphors allowed, babe."

"Fuck you."

"Now *that's* my dainty cousin." Gino looked distractedly over his shoulder. "I got a sick guy behind the bar and a botched delivery on the phone. Feel better. Whatever it is, it ain't worth it. Catch you later, okay?"

As Gino raced back behind the bar, Reina felt her cell phone ring. She glanced at the screen.

BYRON.

Quickly she flipped it open. "Are you here?"

"No, I'm driving to Penn Station!" his voice crackled. "Sorry. I was at Blowback, but I had to . . . move my car. It was double parked. Anyway . . ."

Reina heard a high-pitched moan in the background. *"Byron?"* she said.

"That's not . . . I mean, *I'm* not . . . it's a long story," Byron replied. "Not what you think. *Way* not what you think."

"As long as you're all right. You sounded awful over the phone earlier. I could barely hear you, but it sounded like something was wrong."

"No, everything's just fine. . . ." Byron's voice drifted off, and then he said, softer, "Actually, Reina, it's not. Do you have a minute? Because the reason I'm in this car—"

"Holy shit . . ." Reina was no longer listening. In the middle of the dance floor, a short-haired girl in a stupid floral dress was peddling pills out in the open. "Byron, can I call you back later? Someone is selling drugs like they're Girl Scout cookies."

"*What?*" Byron shouted. "Is it a she?"

"Yes."

"Really short hair, kind of pretty, dressed like she just blew in from the farm?"

"Yes."

"Oh, fuck. I know her, Reina. Her name is MC. She came to the club with me."

"She was your *date*? Doesn't she know *anything*? There are cops all over this place after that *New York* article. If Gino sees her she is dead meat."

"Reina. Listen to me—"

"I'll call you back, Byron."

Reina snapped the phone shut and moved toward the girl. She was trying to do a deal with a tall beehive-haired transvestite who looked like Amy Winehouse.

"Are they good?" Beehive asked flirtatiously.

"Better than good," the girl replied with a wink. "The best. Ever."

Beehive put one arm around her, holding out a wad of

cash with the other. "Can I get a personal guarantee?"

"Hey!" Reina shouted, but there were still too many people in her way.

"Looks like a fair price to me," the girl said, snatching the cash and stuffing it into her bra. "And how!"

Beehive raised a theatrical hand to a rocky jaw. "Did you actually say, 'And how'? Oh, I think I'm going to faint."

Reina was close enough now to grab the girl's arm. "What are you doing? You can't do that here! There are cops around."

"Jealousy is a harsh mistress," Beehive hissed.

"Fuck off," Reina snapped, pulling the girl away.

"Oh, jeez, did you ever see an uglier girl in your life?" the girl said with a giggle.

Reina cringed. "Um, is your name MC?"

"How did you know that?" the girl asked.

Holding on to the girl's arm, Reina led her toward the women's room. "Come with me. We need to talk."

34

BYRON
1:27 A.M.

Another fifty.

Byron whooped aloud at the feel of his second fifty-dollar bill, as he watched André and Yuki disappear, a little wobblier than they had been outside the club, down the steps of Penn Station.

This one had been just as easy as the first. At the drop-off, André had seemed ecstatic. His first question had been "How much do I owe you?" And in a triumph of sense over propriety, Byron had beaten back the urge to say *But you already paid me!* and blurted out, "Fifty."

The amount had just popped into his head. It was a New York amount. It bore no relationship to any rational cost analysis. There was a vague feeling that a fair amount of the first payment had gone to expenses, so a second charge of an equal amount was reasonable and appropriate.

And they had paid it.

Byron tucked it into his pocket and pulled away. He had a little over seventy-five now. Not enough to pay off Waits, but it was a good start.

He was about to call Reina back, to pick up where they had left off. He was dying to let *someone* know— and to find out out what had happened to MC. But as he pulled away from the curb, he spotted a group of twenty-somethings emerging from the glass doors. The first one out, a red-haired girl, went running to the curb, waving her arms.

"Hi! Where are you heading?" Byron called out.

The girl grinned, turning to her friends. "Guys? *Guys, come on, we have a ride!*"

Byron loaded them in and drove them clear down to the Palladium.

They were louder and more fun than André and Yuki. They had a CD of some band their friend belonged to, and Byron played it as they chattered all the way there.

"That'll be thirty," he said, figuring he'd give them a break for good behavior.

After a quick gathering of funds among the group,

they gave him thirty-five and even threw in a couple of kisses.

One hundred and ten total.

What a gig.

He took a threesome from the Palladium to the Empire Diner near Twenty-third Street. A miniskirted, Afroed transvestite who changed outfits in the backseat and emerged a business-suited yuppie on West and Morton. A Wall Street type with two female companions who somehow managed to use three condoms.

He ran two red lights and nearly got front-ended on Third Avenue, but his skills were improving by the block. With his profits he decided to upgrade his customers' experience with a fancier selection of condoms, assorted snacks, and—for the car—a spray bottle of Febreze.

At the corner of First Avenue and Sixth Street, Byron took his first break. The car's clock read 1:55. He was amazed at how much ground he could cover in a half hour. Taking out his cash to count, he kept the money low and out of sight of the street. Around him, spiky postpunks and middle-aged Indian-restaurant customers milled around happily ignoring one another among the open outdoor shops.

He was reaching four hundred dollars when a girl peeked in and said, "Can you help me?"

Byron stashed the money in his pocket. The girl's breath reeked of alcohol, and her eyes were slits. She had a thick head of hair that looked blond under a not-too-skillful orange dye job. Despite the tongue piercing, studs, and tight black clothes, she sent out strong Midwesterner signals. "Sure," he said tentatively. "Where are you going?"

"Avenue A and Eleventh? I gotta get away from somebody. I don't have much money. Wait." She reached into a pocket and pulled out two dollars.

Byron sighed. "Keep it. Get in."

"*Really?* You are soooo sweet!"

She plopped into the backseat, smiling at him into the rearview mirror. But the moment he turned the ignition, she was fast asleep.

35

WAITS
October 18, 1:34 A.M.

"Do you know when you're going to find your bag?" the coat room girl asked. "'Cause Bentley says I'm not supposed to allow anyone back here."

"You didn't see a black shoulder bag, kind of thick and heavy?" Waits asked.

Where was it?

The girl rolled her eyes. "Well, that narrows it down to maybe a hundred bags...."

Was Reina lying? Was she sending him on some fucked-up wild-goose chase, to teach him some kind of lesson? He'd been looking for twenty minutes. This place was total chaos.

"Do you know Reina Sanchez?" Waits asked.

"Uh-huh. Gino's cousin, right?" the girl said.

"Have you seen her?"

"Nuh-uh."

"If you do, tell her Waits wants to see her."

"Uh-kay."

Waits ran back out of the room. He would pull Reina in here, make her find the fucking bag herself.

The club was more crowded than ever, the music cranked to ear-shattering volume. Waits made his way to the bar, where he'd last seen Reina.

He didn't have much hope of finding her. If she was scamming him, she'd be gone by now.

And Ianuzzi would find him.

Unless . . .

Cam.

The big moose owed him. Waits would have to get his money from Cam, and now.

Waits pulled out his cell, sent him a text message, and prayed the asshole would get back to him before Waits was being loaded into the trunk of a black Hummer.

36

JIMMY
October 18, 1:34 A.M.

"Son of a bitch!" The limo driver leaned on his horn, careening onto the entrance ramp of the Saw Mill Parkway. "Look at this guy! Ha! The trick to driving in New York City—don't blink. You have to assert yourself!"

Jimmy clutched the rear armrest of the limo. A Volvo sedan was trying to merge into traffic from a ramp to the right, but the limo driver wasn't letting him in. He sped up, narrowing the gap to inches with the car in front of him.

Cam moaned, holding his side. "Slow down, Richard! I'm in a fragile state and you're making me sick."

"It's Ripley," the driver said. "*Wait your turn, you fucker!* Not you kids, the driver. Ripley. Rip . . . Lee. You know, like, Believe It or Not?"

Jimmy's fingers were frozen white. It was his first time back on the highway since the accident. It had taken forever to get Cam released from the hospital. All Jimmy wanted to do was get home, but Cam was dead set on finding Byron. Somehow.

The woods seemed to have changed since the last time he'd seen them. Behind every passing tree, in every shadow, he saw deer. Calculating. Waiting. Huddled in their hidden deer terrorist cells, waiting for one brave four-legged martyr to commit the ultimate sacrifice and jump out onto the road.

The driving habits of Ripley were not making things any easier. People who drove Toyota Highlander limos were not supposed to be like this.

BEEEEP!

Cam's cell was ringing again.

"Tell them I'm not home," Cam muttered, pulling out his phone and silencing it. "Tell them I'm dead."

Jimmy glanced at the screen:

where ru????—w

"It's 'w' again," Jimmy said. "Who is that—and why are we doing this?"

Leaning across the backseat, Cam squinted at the screen. "It's Waits."

"The guy with the sunglasses, who hangs out by the school? You *know* that guy?"

"Know him? He's the reason we're here."

Jimmy put the phone down. "What do you mean?"

"Oh, Jesus." Cam sank back into the seat and let out a long, slow breath. "Jimmy, you are so fucking naive. We were going to the party to make a sale, so I could pay Waits back."

Jimmy's mouth fell open. "Drugs?"

"No, you douche—aspirin."

The words caught in Jimmy's throat. Drugs. They had been carrying contraband—in the car. Which he had been driving. Without a license.

The mind reeled.

His head spun momentarily, and everything around him receded—the trees, the hidden kamikaze deer—all blotted out by the explosion of bad memories into fragments slowly rearranging into something worse.

"I owed Waits some cash," Cam went on, "and he called in the loan. He needed to pay his people. I had heard about this party, so I told him I would unload some pills, sell them at a huge markup. I wasn't expecting *this* to happen."

"So that's why you wanted my money?" Jimmy couldn't believe what he was hearing. *"To pay Waits?"*

"It's an emergency," Cam said. "Byron and I were supposed to split the seller's percentage and give the profit back to—"

"Byron knew about this?" Jimmy blurted out.

Cam nodded. "He was too scared to drive, and I can't drive worth shit. So he figured he'd ask you."

"And neither of you told me?" The last few days were flashing through his mind in a new harsh light. "And that scene outside the Speech room after school . . . when you stuck up for me . . . that was all a setup, to get me to drive while keeping this whole thing a secret?"

"Fuck no, I am not smart enough to do that. That was Byron's call. I didn't care one way or the other if he told you about the plan. He thought that if you knew, you wouldn't agree to go."

"Right," Jimmy said. "And then none of this would have happened!"

Cam yawned. "Dude, that's why I'm telling you. Now maybe you won't feel so bad for what you did to me when I was unconscious. I mean, that wasn't a real stellar moment in the moral history of the world either."

Jimmy sat back, trying to sift it all. "You both led me into this. You lied. You made me an accessory to a crime I didn't even know I was committing."

"I guess deep down inside, babycakes, we're all . . . basically . . . shit."

Cam was mumbling now, his head lolling to one side. As he dozed off, Jimmy fought back the urge to ask Ripley to stop the car so he could get out and walk home from Riverdale.

BEEEEP!

The phone was lighting up again.

Jimmy picked it up and looked at the screen:

cam u slanty-eye mfokker where ru with my $????—w

The fucking nerve.

Did Waits have any idea? Did he know what had happened, how many lives had been screwed up tonight—by his stupid deal-gone-wrong?

The message seemed to be glowing at him defiantly, daring him to answer.

Cam was starting to snore.

And Jimmy began to type:

jimmy here. bad accident. cam is dead.

37

REINA
October 18, 1:39 A.M.

"I—I'm really sorry," MC said, dabbing Reina's eyes with toilet paper. "I didn't know you knew these guys so well."

"He told you that name—Cam? He said Cam was . . . ?"

MC nodded. "I didn't . . . I wasn't sure if he was just, you know . . . goofing, or making up a name."

"Cam is real," Reina said softly. "Oh God, no wonder Byron sounded so upset when he called me at work."

The bathroom tiles were swimming in Reina's vision. Why hadn't Byron told her the story over the phone?

Cam was dead.

Dead.

You thought of someone—his laugh, his smell, the

way his hair fall across his face—and then that word just wipes it all away. Like it never existed.

And why? Over a drug deal? Cam?

Byron?

"It doesn't make sense," Reina said. "Those guys weren't like that."

"I'm sorry," MC replied, tears now streaming down her face. "If I'd known . . . if I'd only known how serious this all was. I didn't mean to do what I was doing. I got carried away. And Byron never told about Cam until he'd already split . . ."

The girl's words were diffusing into the air, weightless and without meaning. Soon she stopped talking altogether and put her arm around Reina's shoulder.

They sat like that, silent on the bathroom floor, as clubbers came and went, no one noticing a thing was wrong.

38

WAITS
October 18, 1:45 A.M.

He sagged against the bar, trying to make sense of it all.

He stared the message for what seemed like the hundredth time:

jimmy here. bad accident. cam is dead.

This wasn't supposed to happen. It had started as a goof. It was fucking *aspirin.*

Waits began to return Jimmy's text message but didn't know what to say. He was feeling sick, his mind firing and misfiring with memories, images.

Can you see the little boy's face—oh yes, indeedy, he is soooo scared. Iz was talking to him, but his voice was muddy and his face was leering, his smile revealing teeth sharp as knives. *Ha-ha, you have no idea! The boy isn't me,*

it's YOU, my child, and his beady eyes are following those
dollah bills, all the way to the Big Time. Just like yours, you
little prick . . .

Out. He had to get out. He would make up for this. If
it took him the rest of his life. He began to text back, but
his fingers were shaking:

what happened???? where r

"Yo, you . . . dude . . ." came a vaguely familiar voice.

Waits looked up to see the coat-check babe walking
past. "I found ya girlfriend. She's in the bathroom. Crying."

It took a moment for Waits to realize what she was
talking about. *"Reina?"*

"Yeah."

Waits shoved the phone into his pocket and hurried
to the bathroom. As he pushed the door open, he saw
Reina sitting on the floor, arm in arm with a tough-looking
chick in a flower-print dress. He hadn't taken Reina for
being that type.

"This is the *women's* room," Reina murmured, her face
streaked with tears. "Can't you read?"

"This is a club, it doesn't matter," Waits shot back.
Tears always got to him, but not now. Now everything
was different. Lives had been ruined, and now Waits *had*
to get out. The only thing in his way was Reina. "I don't

mean to interrupt, but where is my shoulder bag? It's not in the coatroom."

Reina spun around to face him. "I never said it was."

"Don't play with me, Reina. Do you know what happened tonight?"

Reina's eyes spat ice. "I'm not sure if I heard that correctly, Waits. Are you referring to the fact that you killed Cam?"

The walls began to tilt, and then to spin. "I did not kill Cam," he said. "I had nothing to do with—"

Reina turned into one of the stalls. A girl and a guy came scrambling out, looking disoriented and vaguely coitus interruptus. From inside, Reina called out, "You want your shoulder bag, Waits? You want your money? *Here's your fucking money!"* She emerged with his bag over her shoulder but marched right past him.

He reached for her, but she shook loose. "Reina? Where are you going?"

Waits ran after her as she barreled through the throng, pushing aside dancers, causing drinks to crash to the floor.

In the middle of the club, under a pulsing red light, she turned to face him. By now, a circle of mildly stunned people had gathered around them. "You know, Waits," she said with a disarmingly calm smile, "I really like this shoulder bag. It must have cost you a fortune. Do you think I could keep it?"

"Yes, Reina, it's all yours," Waits said, walking toward her patiently, not trusting the tone of her voice. "Just as soon as I get my stuff out."

"Oh, that's no problem," Reina replied. "Let me do it for you!"

She unzipped the bag and turned it upside down.

"What are you doing?" Waits shouted.

"Woooo-HOOOOOO!"

People were running toward them from all directions as masses of cash flew out across the dance floor. They were diving, grasping, laughing. Reina stood among them, tears running down her face.

This was not happening.

He was a dead man.

39

BYRON
October 18, 1:59 A.M.

"No. No. Stick your head *out* of the car," Byron said. "Do it on the *sidewalk*."

He held the girl's shoulders as she struggled out of the backseat and onto Eleventh Street. Her name was Cleo, he'd gotten that much out of her. And the last thing he wanted to do at this point was become an amusing part of the gazillionth Wisconsin girl's *Sex and the City* blog.

Still, he felt bad for her as she threw up into the gutter, sobbing. "I'm—I'm usually not like this . . . ohhhh, I'm sooo sooo sorrryyyy. Did I mess up your car?"

"Nope," Byron said, lifting her to her feet and putting an arm around her shoulder.

"I have money upstairs," she said. "I can pay you."

He began walking with her toward a dark tenement building. "Don't even think of it. Let's get you to bed."

"I don't want to have sex."

"Don't worry, I don't want to either."

"So you're gay?"

"No! Look, I just want you to be safe. And home."

"You are the best man ever!" She was struggling with a set of keys now, forcing one and then another into the front door, until it finally pushed open. "I'm on the second floor. Apartment 2E."

Byron helped her up the stairs and into her apartment. It was one room, crammed with boxes and clothes strewn all over. In the center was a queen-size bed, relatively clear, and Byron set her gently down on it. "Okay, look," he said, "whatever happened to you tonight, just don't worry about it. It'll be better in the morning."

Cleo smiled at him, her lips swollen and her eyes peering from behind a scrim of sweat-soaked orange hair. "What about you?"

"Me?" Byron cocked his head. "I'm great."

"Great . . . ," the girl said, her eyes closing as she snuggled into a pillow. "It's great that you're great . . . but you don't sound great . . . so if you want to talk . . ."

Byron exhaled and turned away. He was exhausted and achy and tense. He hadn't had a chance to tell Reina anything—and who knows what happened between her and MC.

Cleo was fast asleep. But her invitation to talk was too hard to resist. The whole crazy night was all bottled up inside him.

"I—I don't know what's happening to me," he began rambling, taking comfort in the sound of his own words. "The market, I guess. I was burned on a margin call—I know, stupid move. So, you know, desperate times . . . I broker this fifty-fifty drug deal with some jock in our school. I even trick a good bud into driving us to a party upstate—and he doesn't even know the plan. But we hit this deer, total the car, and now the jock . . . Cam . . . is dead. I hide the drugs inside the deer's mouth. My friend and I go to the party but the cops take him and I drive back to the scene, just as this weird chick is putting the deer in her pickup. I follow her and when she realizes what I'm doing, she thinks, hey, cool, let's sell the drugs together, at Blowback. So we go there and I see the dealer, I freak, and I run outside. I spot this tow truck—but when I move my double-parked car, this couple jump in, thinking I'm a cab, and they pay me a hundred bucks. I figure I can keep that up all night, to make my nut.

So that's what I'm doing—running an illegal car service in a stolen car to pay back a drug dealer for a botched sale in which my friend was killed and his car totaled."

Saying it all just made it worse, the night's horror darkening with every sentence, and Byron began to cry.

Cleo sat up and gave him a soft kiss on the cheek. "That sucks. If it's true."

Startled, Byron flinched. "You heard me?"

"It sounds like a novel, except you can't make up this shit," she said, fading back onto the bed, her words slurry. "I've got people chasing after me, too."

"The thing is, if I get enough money, it'll all be over."

"It's never enough. A shitty bargain's a shitty bargain. I think . . . um, stop driving, dude. Go back to the guy . . . give him whatever. Tell him you're out of the deal, Byron. You're too good for this."

"You think?" Byron said.

"I know."

Byron leaned into her and gave her a big hug. Her clothes were wet and she didn't smell particularly fresh, but it felt good. "How did you get so smart?"

"If I was so smart, you wouldn't have had to drive me home." Cleo smiled, her eyes closed. "I'd kiss you for real, but I have puke breath."

Byron stood, smiling. "I'll take a rain check."

He pulled open the door and left. As he walked down the stairs, he realized he'd left the car running and parked by a fire hydrant. He ran down and yanked open the front door.

The car was still there, intact, untowed, unticketed, and purring.

Byron took a deep breath of relief. An invitation to steal untaken, in New York City. This was a good omen.

As he jumped into the front seat, he looked up at Cleo's building. Her light was off. He felt the bulge of the envelope in his pocket, thick and oppressive, and imagined it gone. Then he threw the car in gear and edged away from the curb.

He was only vaguely aware of a movement in the rearview mirror. But a moment later he heard both back doors opening.

One last fare wouldn't hurt. "Where to?" he asked, turning around.

In the darkness he thought one of the passengers was offering him an iPod, holding it right up close to his face.

It took a moment to realize it was a knife blade.

"G-g-give us everything you g-g-got," a voice stammered. "Or you ain't going nowhere."

Byron recoiled.

His foot slammed down against the accelerator, and the car careened into the street.

40

JIMMY
October 18, 2:07 A.M.

"Turn left, now! . . . Off COURSE! ReCALculating! . . ."

The limo's GPS device was going haywire. Jimmy could swear it sounded angry.

HONKK! HONNNNNK!

They had stopped in midtown to visit an all-night diner Cam knew about. As a result, Ripley the Driver seemed to want to make up for lost time, and the whole thing had Jimmy pissed. "I thought you wanted to find Byron," he snapped.

"I do," Cam replied, finishing off the last part of a double cheeseburger.

"Then what the fuck did you stop for?"

"I haven't eaten for six hours. These are New York's best burgers!"

"Where did you get your license, Toys "R" Us?" Ripley shouted out the window, then winked happily into the rearview mirror. "You have to show them who is boss."

The car zoomed down the West Side Highway, detouring into the pier service road to avoid lights, emerging into a string of green lights that took them straight from Midtown to the West Village.

"He does this for a living?" Jimmy said, hurtling against the door with the centrifugal force of the Twenty-third Street curve.

"And he's still living," Cam replied with a grim smile.

They hit their first red in front of Chelsea Piers. Once they got through this, they'd be minutes from Blowback.

"You know, Jimmy," Cam continued, "that took balls, what you wrote to Waits. About me being dead. Dang. I never thought I'd say this, dude, but you are pimpin'."

"I finally have something to be proud about in my life."

"So what do we do when we get there? Maybe I should, like, pretend to be a corpse. Put powder on my face or something. You could carry me out. Drop me at Waits's feet. My wrist will fall, ever so limply, upon the floor. And in the hush you say in a choked whisper, 'Good night, sweet prince . . .'"

"That is so gay, Cam."

"It's fucking Shakespeare!"

"Impressive. I thought you were still working your way through *One fish two fish red fish blue fish*."

"Suck my dick fish."

"That's more like it. Thought I'd lost you there."

As the car took off, Jimmy felt a light blow to his right bicep. He turned to see Cam, who was giving him a mock grimace, and it brought to mind a phrase from an old Hardy Boys book that Jimmy had never quite understood. "Did you just chuck me on the arm, Frank Hardy?" he asked.

Cam grinned. "'I do believe so,' Frank answered zestily."

Ripley swerved into the right lane, flooring it to get past traffic lined up at Little West 12th. "Whoa, this is it, Ripley!" Jimmy cried out. "You have to turn here!"

EEEEEEEEEE.

They were warping across three lane of traffic now. "It is okay, I will make a U-turn," Ripley announced. "We will need to approach from the downtown side anyway!"

Jimmy and Cam held tight as the driver cut off three cars just in time to get the green at Clarkson, deftly passing a left-turning yellow cab on the right in order to make the U.

HO-O-O-O-ONNNNK!

"Your mother was a gerbil and your father smelled of gooseberries!" Ripley called out the window to the cab driver.

"Whaaaat?" Cam and Jimmy said at the same time.

"To Blowback!" Ripley shouted triumphantly. "No retreat, no surrender!"

"No retreat, no surrender!" they echoed.

All three of them whooped at the top of their lungs as they roared up West Street, past a string of construction sites and clubs.

They were one block away from Blowback when a black Lincoln Town Car ran a red light on Gansevoort Street and came careening directly toward them.

41

BYRON
October 18, 2:14 A.M.

Byron slammed on the brakes. He hadn't seen the red light. Or the Highlander. Screaming, he yanked the steering wheel to the right.

"Ho-o-o-o-oly-y-y shi-i-i-i-it!" wailed one of the masked guys in the backseat.

The car lifted upward on the right side. With a sudden lurch and a sickening crunch, it smacked against the dark blue limo, which skidded sharply away, jackknifing across West Street.

There, the cars in all three downtown lanes scattered like bowling pins. One of the cars smashed through a wooden guard rail and a cement planter. People on the pier dove for cover. The vehicle was an enormous black

Hummer that seemed to flout the laws of physics as it flipped over on its side.

With a sickening, drawn-out crunch, the black Hummer slid into the darkness of the Hudson River.

HONNNNNNNNK!

Byron floored it again, taking the turn in the clear. People in front of Blowback were diving onto the sidewalk. In the rearview mirror he saw his two attackers jostling to sit up again.

He yanked the wheel to the left, right, left. As he'd done all the way across town.

This time the knife wielders weren't falling. They were still upright.

Right. Sharp.

The car skipped the curb. A steel light pole rose up in front of Byron, and he stepped on the brake.

EEEEEEEEEEE . . .

Byron heard a bang. He felt a body blow, head to waist, smacking his head backward, and saw white.

I've been shot.

Around him came the muffled din of shouting, cursing, footsteps, doors opening. Byron felt himself drooping forward. As he fought to breathe, light began seeping into the edges of his peripheral vision. It took a moment to realize the driver's-side airbag was slowly deflating before him.

He felt as if he'd just been kicked by a giant foot. All around him, faces peered in through the windshield. The car's hood now had a sharp pyramidal point in the center, the pole rising out of the top.

He forced himself out of the car, short of breath and doubled over with pain. Someone had pulled open the back door. Inside were the two men in ski masks, unconscious and slumped over each other.

The surrounding gawkers seemed to be frozen, staring at Byron as if he were a vampire. He leaned into the backseat and pulled off their masks. One of them was a pimply guy, probably no more than fourteen. The other was a girl about the same age with braces.

Their chests were rising and falling, their pulses flowing. The knife had fallen to the floor, and Byron carefully picked it up. It was plastic.

"Oh, fuck . . . ," he murmured.

On the floor was a mesh-fabric Pioneer Supermarket bag hidden in the shadow. He lifted it and looked inside.

The contents were impossible to see without turning the bag toward the streetlight. As he did, crumpled little portraits of Washington, Franklin, and Jackson stared up at him.

Lots of them.

42

REINA
October 18, 2:15 A.M.

"Get your hands off that!"

"Yo, I found it first!"

A fist, meant for someone else, headed for Reina's face. She jumped back, trying to get as far away as she could from the center of the dance floor.

Spilling the bag was an unfathomably stupid thing to do.

The word had spread. Now people were leaping on each other's backs, moshing, screaming, fighting, stuffing bills into their pockets and shoes and mouths, whooping as if it were a big game. Waits was in the midst of it, threatening everyone in earshot, grabbing at money like a wild animal.

Where was Gino? When you stepped away from the melee, it was hard to know what was happening. It didn't look so different from dancing. Which was a good thing, she guessed. Maybe it would all clear itself up. No cops meant no trouble for Gino.

Reina wished she could roll back the minutes and do it over again, control her temper. She backpedaled, catching a glimpse of MC in the crowd. She called out her name but saw that MC was being pulled toward the bar by the Amy Winehouse clone.

As Reina neared the door, she heard another commotion. Outside, on the street, people were shouting about something else. Police cars were closing in from all around, and she could see an SUV stopped diagonally across the road, blocking traffic.

She ducked back in. This sucked. Big-time. The cops would close the place down. She had to get to Gino now.

As she headed back to the crowd, someone plowed into her from the left, catching her off balance. Reina screamed, tumbling downward among a sea of stomping feet.

Another body fell on top of her, smothering her.

"Get off!" she screamed, pushing upward.

"Reina?"

She sat up, staring into a face of a maniac who knew her name, his hair matted to one side, his eyes red, and his face cut and bloodied past recognition.

43

CAM
October 18, 2:17 A.M.

"I love this," Cam said to Jimmy as he limped toward the front of Blowback. "I love this a lot."

"Did you see that car that turned over?" Jimmy said. "Someone might have gotten killed. *We* almost got killed!"

"It was a Hummer," Cam said. "Those things are built for that kind of shit. I'm not sure about the dude driving that Lincoln. What was *he* smoking?"

"*He's* the one who almost killed us!"

"We're alive, Capitalupo. Jesus, you have no fucking sense of adventure."

Cam began mounting the stairs. It hurt like hell to walk and he'd just banged his head against the side of the car in the spinout. He knew he'd lose the next few weeks of the season to injury and might not even play all year.

Still, it didn't matter. It felt good not to be dead. And back in his old stomping grounds. He couldn't wait to see Waits, scare the shit out of him. Money shmoney. He would give Jimmy back his ATM cash. The payment didn't worry him anymore. These things worked out.

They just did.

The bouncer was gone from the front door. It was noisy inside. A wild night. This would be fun.

He pushed open the door.

44

BYRON
October 18, 2:19 A.M.

"Reina, it's *Byron*."

Reina stared at him with disbelief, as if he were scanning a face in a lineup to match something in her memory.

"Is it that bad?" he asked, feeling the cuts that ran along his jaw.

"Yes! What the hell happened to you?"

"Long story." He stood up, clutching a green bag to his chest. "Where's Waits? I need to see Waits. I have to give him something."

"He's—"

But Byron was already racing past her, his eyes intent on the center of the dance floor, where Waits was either dancing or brawling with two women.

Byron staggered forward, thrusting the bag at Waits. "Take this!" he shouted, then dug into his own pocket and pulled the thick wad of cash he'd earned in the car. "And this."

Waits looked at him, flabbergasted. "Who the fuck are you?"

"Take it all, Waits. Take it and go away. Because if I ever see you anywhere near Olmsted again, I'm going to fuck you up. Don't ask me how, but I will find a way."

"Byron?" Waits shook loose from his attackers, dropping a few bills and letting them fight over the loot. "I didn't recognize—"

"Stop it, you're giving me a complex," Byron said.

Waits took Byron's bag but didn't open it. "What's this?"

"What does it look like, you asshole?" Byron said. "It's what you want, right? It's the reason Cam had to sacrifice his life for your fucking greed."

Waits tucked Byron's bills into his pocket and clutched the bag to his chest. "Cam . . . agreed," he said weakly. "No one forced him to buy . . . or you."

"He's *dead*, Waits!" Byron said. "Eighteen years old, his whole life ahead of him—and that's all you can say? 'No one *forced* him'?"

Reina was beside him now, her mouth pulled down in an expression Byron had never seen. "How can you say that, you lowlife piece of shit?"

She was lunging at Waits, who stumbled backward. The crowd, who had managed to pocket the dropped money, stood there watching as she screamed at him, sobbing.

Byron hadn't realized how much Reina had cared about Cam. Cam had an unexpected effect on people.

Byron backed off, tears in his eyes. He had done what he'd intended to do. Cleo was right.

He turned to go, staggering through the throng, feeling the breeze from the front door as it opened and then shut again.

It felt good, the fall air, but it wasn't good enough. It would never be good enough, not for the rest of his life. Not after what he'd done that night.

He began running. Blindly.

As he approached the door full speed, bracing to push it, it swung open.

45

MC
October 18, 2:20 A.M.

"Dang, you're strong for a—"

MC cut herself off. The extremely tall girl with a beehive, who had taken her by the arm and forced her over to the bar, had hair on the back of her hands.

Just her luck that her only customer of the night was a two-hundred-pound transvestite with a complaint.

"I swear, I take these all the time," Beehive said in a deep, rumbly voice, glaring at MC and then over to the bartender, who was rummaging for something behind the bar.

He held up three small plastic bottles. "Which one?"

"That one," Beehive said, pointing to the one on the left, then slapping down onto the bar one of the pills that MC had sold her.

The bartender turned over the little bottle, and MC read the label.

"Holy shit . . ." she said.

She felt herself turning red.

46

WAITS
October 18, 2:22 A.M.

"Reina, I'm sorry," Waits said, wending his way through the crowd, trying to find where Byron had gone. "But I didn't do anything."

Reina followed him, still in a rage. "You set him up! You set both of them up."

"Do you know how Byron got this money?" Waits asked.

"Is that all you can think about? I don't know where he got it! I don't know who did that to his face either."

Waits heard a scream near the front door. "Over there."

Byron was staggering, lurching toward the door. He seemed disoriented. Waits picked up the pace. "I'm worried about him," he said.

"Oh, bullshit," Reina said. "You're worried about how you can get more of it. Just take your blood money, Waits, and stop trying to play good guy."

She didn't understand. She would never understand. "Reina, I don't *want* to do this."

"Do what?"

He stopped, holidng out the bag of cash. "This, Reina—*this*. This fucking business. I hate it. I'm over it. But people are after me. Somewhere in Bay Ridge, they're preparing cement shoes in my size. I'm trying to get out. Can't you understand?"

"Don't you think it's a little late for—"

Reina stopped cold.

As the front door opened, her jaw dropped.

47

BYRON
October 18, 2:23 A.M.

"C—C—C—?"

It was a fucking ghost.

48

REINA
October 18, 2:23 A.M.

"I believe in God."

Tears blurred her vision, as she ran to the door with open arms.

"I believe in God. I believe in God. *I BELIEVE IN GOD!*"

49

CAM
October 18, 2:23 A.M.

Bingo.

50

JIMMY
October 18, 2:23 A.M.

It was chaos.

Reina was all over Cam, sobbing. Byron, who looked as if he'd been in a terrible fight, was grinning like a kid on wobbly legs.

And Waits's face, for the first time he'd noticed, was arranging into a look of something resembling surprise, as if there was actually something in the world he had never seen before.

Cam just made this kind of stuff happen.

Like the Greeks. Like Orestes.

He wondered if he could work this into a dramatic five-minute piece.

Nahh.

51

WAITS

October 18, 2:23 A.M.

"Holy shit . . ."

He was alive.

Fucking alive!

The text message was a lie. Cam had been dicking around with his brain.

Cam looked a little banged up, although not as much as Byron did.

Relief, which had washed over him at the sight of Cam, was now hardening into anger. Who the fuck did he think he was? Was this his idea of a joke?

"Heyyyy, Waits, you been shopping at Pioneer?" bellowed the conquering hero, gesturing toward the bag of money. "Get any good deals in the drug aisle?"

Waits could feel his face turning red.

Keep cool.

"It's good to see you, Cam," he said.

"Look, dude, I got into a little mess up in Disturbia. I couldn't do the job I set out to do, you know?"

Waits nodded. "That's no problem, Cam. I'm not expecting—"

"But I've had some time to think, with my homey J, and I feel really bad about what we did to him. Deception is bad. And that's partially my bad, but yours too. In fact, I feel bad about this whole thing, Waits."

Before Waits could answer, a hand came flying out of nowhere, connecting with the left side of his face.

"You son of a bitch!"

He spun around, grabbing his ear. The club was going around in circles. It was Reina's friend, the one in the bathroom. "What the fuck?"

"Whoa," came Cam's voice.

The girl was a blaze of sinew and white-and-floral pattern. She moved like a guy, knocking Waits to the floor and straddling him as if he were a roped steer.

It hurt like hell.

"Get off me!" Waits shouted. *"What is wrong with you?"*

A group was gathering about them, cheering.

The girl rose to her feet, pulling Waits up by his shirt collar. With her other hand, she was pulling an envelope out of her dress. "Here's what's wrong," she said, holding the envelope out and turning it over.

A small sea of white fell out of the envelope. Little pills clattered to the floor, rolling away.

Byron was racing toward her now. *"No! What the fuck are you doing, MC?"*

"Is that her name—MC?" Cam was asking. "Dang, she's hot. Does she know who I am?"

"You think she's hot?" Reina asked.

"Don't bother picking them up, Byron, unless you have a really big headache," MC said. "Because they're aspirin!"

52

BYRON
October 18, 2:24 A.M.

"Aspirin?" Byron watched in amazement as the pills rolled away.

Reina shook her head. "Aspirin . . ."

Cam smiled at MC. "Unbuffered. They're cheaper."

"Those drugs you gave me, Byron, the ones you hid in the *deer*?" MC said. "This son of a bitch had given you aspirin!"

"You hid it in the *deer*?" Jimmy said.

"It's a long story," Byron said.

"Someone inside recognized the pills, after I sold some to her," MC said. "I mean, *him*. She . . . *he* showed them to the bartender, who had a whole bottle full of them—same exact markings."

Cam nodded. "I knew that. I bought those pills. At Rite Aid."

"Whaat?" Jimmy, Reina, and MC said at the same time.

"I owed Waits," Cam said. "He needed cash. I told him I could fool these suburban kids—I could sell them aspirin. I was bragging on my own ass. He just took me up on it."

"Holy shit," Byron said. "What if someone at the party would have figured it out?"

Jimmy was staring at him, head cocked to one side. "I can't believe you hid aspirin in the *deer.*"

"If they'd figured it out," Waits said, grimacing from the pressure MC was applying to his arm, "you would split. No harm done. They wouldn't miss the cash. You don't know them, you'll never see them again."

"There's a word for that," Byron said. "I think it's called stealing."

He felt light-headed. This entire night—this whole ordeal . . . He had chased a dead deer on a pickup, spent a whole night driving people around to raise money, nearly got himself killed . . . for *aspirin*?

"Will you let me go!" Waits said, trying to pry himself loose from MC. "You're a fucking animal."

MC grinned, turning to the others. "What should I do?"

"Smash his head!" cried someone from the crowd.

Byron noticed Waits reaching backward for his Pioneer bag, which had fallen in the tumble.

"Yo, Reina!" a voice cried from the crowd, which had now gathered around them in a circle. A burly guy with a receding hairline and a gold chain around his massive neck burst through the people and stopped. "Jesus. Do you know these people?"

"Hi, Gino," Reina said. "I do. This is kind of my fault. In a way."

"The place is trashed, there are cops all over the street, cars totaled, including one in the river. . . . Do you know how much this is going to cost us?" Gino said.

Byron picked up the green bag and handed it to him. "This ought to help."

"Noooo!" Waits yelled, lunging toward him.

"You ripped my dress!" MC shouted. "I can't believe you ripped my dress."

Now the crowd was parting again, and two men stepped through. The younger guy had the toughness of an ex-jock not yet gone to seed. The other guy, though, looked like he'd just stepped out of a Popeye cartoon. "I am Officer Timothy Scranton, and this is Officer Bruno Barnes," the old guy said to Gino.

"Do you see who I see, Scrotum?" said Bruno.

"Use my real name in mixed company, will you please, you candy-ass bastard?" Scrotum shot back, then turned to Waits. "We thought you would like to know that you will not be seeing us again."

"All good things come to pass, Duncan," Bruno said.

Reina smiled at Waits. "Your name is *Duncan*?"

"What the fuck are you guys talking about?" Waits asked.

"Perhaps you would like to join us," Scrotum said, gesturing to the front door.

MC released Waits with one final sadistic arm twist.

The two undercover cops began moving to the front door. Byron followed close behind with Jimmy and Cam, as Reina and MC pulled Waits along behind them.

Floodlights had been set up along West Street, shining out toward the river. All traffic had been stopped, a squadron of police cars parked every which way, lights flashing.

A crane was lifting a black Hummer out of the river, as a team of medics strapped three men to gurneys.

"Ianuzzi . . . ," Waits murmured. "And Feets."

"Fine gentlemen, purveyors of controlled substances," Bruno said.

"Fuckheads," Scrotum added. "They been hiding out for a long time, but the DA's got a rap sheet they'll never break. He's the last of that family to fall."

Byron glanced at Waits. He looked about ten years younger. Almost like a normal person. "You mean, that's it? I don't have to—"

"Pay up?" Bruno said. "Well, let's put it this way. You could take your chances. We could put you in Witness Protection, but if I were you, I'd just make sure you build a little nest egg. For your own safety."

"I can live with that," Waits said.

MC wiped off his shoulder. "Sorry about that, dude. I got carried away."

"I don't feel a thing," Waits replied.

Reina smiled at Cam. "I'm glad you're all right," she said, her eyes growing moist as she rested her head on his chest.

Cam slowly, tentatively wrapped his arms around her. "Yowza," he murmured under his breath.

Byron glanced at Jimmy, who still looked angry. "Dude. This will never, ever happen again."

Jimmy took a foil-wrapped Wet-Nap out of his pocket. "Take this. Clean your ugly face."

A horn blew, from the area just beyond the ring of

cop cars, and a voice called out, "Are we going to be here all night? I have to eat too!"

"Chill, Ripley!" Cam said. "Can't you see we're having a moment?"

The younger cop turned to his partner. "You know, I think the view of the river is exquisite on an October night, don't you, Officer Scranton?"

"Yes, indeed," the old guy answered as they both turned their backs to MC. "Esi . . . exik . . . esqui . . . really fucking beautiful, Officer Barnes."

53

JIMMY
October 18, 3:49 A.M.

A huge projection flashed across the Blowback ceiling. The DJ was a video geek with a rig, a recent Olmsted grad who did a killer light show on late late Friday nights.

Reina was screaming, her hair falling in front of her face as she danced. Jimmy hadn't seen her this happy in a long time. Byron was grooving on the new girl, MC. Cam was into Reina, and she was into him back. For now everyone seemed just totally pumped.

He had no idea what time it was, but the events of the night already felt like days away. Not that they had really ended. They wouldn't for a long time. He had a court date to explain why he was driving. He'd probably not be able to get his license until he was thirty. Byron's "borrowed" car was on the way to the AAA auto body shop on West Fifty-fourth Street, courtesy of a long, involved call with a guy in Westchester named Frazer. Cam's mom was calling him every few minutes but he kept putting her off. He was also still running up a bill on the hired limo—but at least Ripley had finally stopped bugging him about it and had joined them in the club, dancing with a very large-boned girl who resembled Amy Winehouse.

Waits was headed for the police station. Some questions about past dealings. Bruno and Scrotum weren't going to let him off too easy. Byron knew he should have felt happy about this, but he had a feeling Waits had some good in him and would figure out something constructive to do with his life. It probably would not involve hanging outside Olmsted.

"Dance with me, Jimmy!" Reina said, turning her back to him and swaying violently back and forth, eyeing him over her shoulder.

Jimmy felt a knot in his stomach. He loved to dance. It was the one thing he was good at, outside of school. Reina seemed to be noticing it too.

Suddenly the driver's license problem didn't seem to matter very much.

He danced with Reina, the two of them winding their

way around the vast floor. Above them the images washed over everything, changing the club's color schemes every few minutes—there was a supernova, there a tooth-less guy smiling by a rice paddy. An abandoned circus, a tie-dyed tractor, a deer head on a mantel with a smile painted on it.

Jimmy had to stop to look at that. The eyes, even in the photo, were beautiful.

"Wow," Reina said. "Those eyes are huge."

"Anime-hero huge," Jimmy said.

He smiled.

Deer were like that.

Epilogue

Jimmy Capitalupo, after winning a national forensics trophy for his original oratory entitled *wtf,* turned down a scholarship to Princeton University to attend Georgetown University in Washington, D.C., partly attracted by the city's efficient subway system. He still does not have a driver's license. Or a girlfriend. But he's looking.

Byron Durgin put himself through MIT on revenues from a student-run car service he founded, which had a spotless record for safety and fair prices. He is now CEO of Durgin Rent-a-Car of New York City. He pines for love, and has a particular penchant for short-haired girls in flower-print dresses.

After graduating NYU, **Reina Sanchez** teamed with club owner/restaurateur Gino Sclafani to buy a newly bankrupted Brooklyn coffee shop and develop it into the lucrative nationwide chain Smitté. She broke up with Cam after a long relationship and is considering moving to Washington, D.C., after hearing from Jimmy on Facebook.

Cam Hong left college after his breakup with Reina Sanchez, joined the Peace Corps, and became a practicing Buddhist. He plans to study to become a nuclear physicist or, if that doesn't work out, a weathercaster. At last contact, he owed his father $653.23 for unpaid damages to his car on the night of October 17.

Duncan Waits and **Barbara "MC" Reemer** were married in a civil ceremony in New York City, where he sells title insurance and she is studying taxidermy. They hope one day to move in with her father, the beloved ex-caretaker of a Westchester mansion inherited by him after the untimely death of the owners in a hunting accident. In the meantime they live in Brooklyn and have seventeen pets. Their neighbors hate them.

About the Author

Peter Lerangis lives in New York City. Really.

HERE'S A LOOK AT A NOVEL THAT'S SURE TO MAKE YOU SAY, "wtf!"

Pre-game

I decided for about the hundredth time tonight that I'm not going to Cassandra Castillo's spring break barter party.

Then I changed my mind, because, fuck it: I'm seventeen, lonely, and horny. If I bailed on the party, not only would Coop and Ben never forgive me, but I'd have nothing else to do tonight that didn't involve a bottle of hand lotion and a crusty sock of Catholic shame.

Friday night. I was sitting in a booth at a greasy dive with my best friends, Coop and Ben, praying for the finger of God to wipe us and the whole stupid town of Rendview off the map so that I wouldn't have to make a decision about Cassie's party. The problem wasn't the party. It was the hostess of the party and the fact that, for the first time since freshman year, she was single. And not just single. Newly single. In fact, she had barely been free of the shackles of monogamy for an entire week. But if I was going to make my move, I couldn't afford to waste time.

Coop interrupted my Cassie-filled daydreams by asking me and Ben a totally irrelevant question. "Who'd play you in a movie about your life?" Coop flashed a grin, unleashing the dimples from which no teenage girl is immune. Which sucks for them because he's totally into dudes. One dude in particular.

Ben snatched a fry off my plate and shoved it into his mouth without so much as a please or thank you. Which is how Ben is. Love him or loathe him, you don't get between him and a french fry. Not if you value your fingers. "Definitely Jake Gyllenhaal," Ben said.

"Just because he plays you," Coop said, "doesn't mean you get to bang him."

"Unless he's a method actor."

"You are pretty good at fucking yourself," I said, and pulled my plate of limp fries out of his reach.

Ben kissed Coop on the cheek and said to me, "You'd be played by a Muppet. And the movie would be called: *Simon Cross and the Blue Balls of Destiny*." Ben cracked up at his own joke and slid out of the booth to go talk to friends at another table.

Coop, Ben, and I had been best friends since grade school, when we all got stuck at the same lunch table with Phil Bluth. Banding together was the only way to protect our precious pudding cups from Phil's grabby hands. We were the Three Musketeers. The Three Amigos. Peter, Ray, and Egon. Until junior year of high school, when Ben and Coop coupled up. I thought it was great that they had fallen in lust and all that sappy bullshit, but I often felt like the third wheel of a trike that longed to be a big, bad, two-wheeled bicycle, riding off into the sunset, leaving me to pedal solo on the lonely road to Loserville. Population: me.

"Earth to Simon." Coop snapped his fingers in front of my eyes and brought me back to our sticky booth in the middle of Gobbler's, which is famous for being one of the few places in town that won't immediately call the cops on kids for hanging out, and not at all famous for their lousy burgers. Rendview is a sleepy beach town on the east coast of Florida, and there isn't much to do except eat, sleep, surf, and get drunk. That last item was on everyone's agenda for the evening. Gobbler's was wall-to-wall with my classmates. It was the last Friday of spring break and we were all getting ready to migrate to Cassie's house for a night of balls-to-the-wall teenage rebellion.

Despite the fact that I couldn't wait to graduate from the soul-rotting drudgery of high school, I felt a bond with some of these guys, forged from our years of shared suffering. Suffering that would come to an end at our imminent graduation.

"Ben's only messing with you," Coop said.

"I'm a loser," I said. "A seventeen-year-old virgin. I'm going to graduate in a couple of months, go to community college, and end up sleeping with someone like Mrs. Elroy because I repulse girls my own age with my wit and charm and concave chest."

"Don't sell yourself short," Coop said. "Mrs. Elroy was hot back in the nineteen twenties."

"Lucky me." I picked at one of my fries but tossed it down without eating it. "Even if I did manage to bag her, she'd end up showing me the door before I've had a chance to say, 'I swear it doesn't usually happen that fast'—though who am I kidding, it always happens that fast—because her husband will be home any moment and, oh wait, I think that's him now. Better jump out the window. Naked. Yeah, good times."

Coop laughed into his napkin, and I thought for a minute that he was going to choke, which would have served him right. But the bastard had the nerve to cough and catch his breath again. "It's not that dire. There are plenty of girls that'll do you."

"If you say Aja Bourne, I'm going to punch your face off."

"No," Coop said. "We'll find you a nearsighted girl who likes to binge drink."

"I'd prefer something less date-rapey."

"Who's date-raping whom?" Ben asked as he slid back into the booth, throwing his ropey arm around Coop's shoulders. Ben is always in motion, even when he's sitting still. It's like his molecules can't stop bouncing around. Our school had suggested he go on ADHD meds back in eighth grade, but Ben's mom had told them where they could stick their pills. Four years later, Ben is about to graduate with a free ride to MIT. Guess he showed them.

"I'm not date-raping anyone," I said, loudly enough that a couple of kids at the closest tables turned to gawk.

Ben was eyeballing my fries, so I pushed the soggy leftovers across the table. "Maybe more girls would be into you if you weren't so obvious about your Cassie fetish," he said

"Ixnay on the Assie-Cay," Coop said. I hate how he and Ben treat me like a feral monkey who's going to fling his shit at them every time they mention Cassie's name. Sure, I'm totally into the girl, but I'm not obsessed.

"The party is at Cassie's house," I said. "She was going to come up eventually." I did my best to keep my voice even and calm. I'd had plenty of practice.

Here's the lowdown on the Cassie situation: I love her. The feeling isn't, technically, mutual. Maybe, possibly, somewhere deep, deep down where even she doesn't know they exist, Cassie might have some sweaty feelings for me, but it's highly unlikely. Girls like Cassie don't go for skinny geeks like me, in spite of my awesome hair.

And that should have been the end of it, except that freshman year, I'd done the unthinkable. I'd asked her out. And she'd said yes. We'd gone on one date and I'd nearly kissed her but—

"Are you thinking about mini-golf again?" Ben asked. Without waiting for an answer, he slapped me across the face so hard that spit flew out of my mouth and hit the wall. Someone whispered, "Cat fight," from a nearby table, and hissed.

Coop and I gaped at Ben. "Negative reinforcement," Ben said. "Every time he thinks about, talks about, or looks at Cassie, I'll slap him."

I put my hand to my cheek and wiggled my jaw. "You, sir, are a douchenozzle."

"I could punch you in the balls instead." Ben made a fist and leaned forward.

Coop held Ben back. "Can we save the ball punching for later?"

"Or never," I said.

"But Ben has a point," Coop said. "Just yesterday you were going on and on about how the party is the perfect chance for you to tell Cassie you love her and to finally kiss her, finishing what you started at Pirate Chang's."

Ben gulped some of my soda. "That was years ago, buddy. Time to move on. Your crush, while adorable, is starting to curdle. Pretty soon you're going to be that creepy guy who lives in his parents' basement, wallpapering his bedroom with old pictures of the girl he can't get over."

My friends had a point, but that didn't stop my brain from churning out scenario after scenario—imagined histories of what my life might have been like if I'd kissed Cassie that night instead of letting her get away. I feel about Cassie the way Coop feels about Ben. And even though I know that Cassie doesn't feel the same way about me, I've hoped. For years, every time she talked to me, every time she smiled in my direction, I hoped.

"Let's say you do make a play for Cassie tonight," Coop said. "And, for the record, I'm not saying I think it's a good idea. What about Eli?"

"Don't egg him on," Ben said. "Simon's got as much chance of scoring with Cassie as he has of scoring with me."

"Wow," I said. "Thanks for the support."

"I'm not trying to be a dick—"

"It comes more naturally to some," I said.

"Simon, listen. Cassie is pretty. She's popular. She's smart as shit. She dates guys like Eli Horowitz. Eli Fucking Horowitz, man."

"She dumped him."

Ben chuckled. "Do you honestly believe that means he won't break you into tiny pieces and then break those pieces into even smaller pieces? Look at him."

We all turned to the far corner where Eli sat alone. He looked like reheated dog shit. Like he hadn't shaved since school let out for spring break. Like he hadn't showered or even bothered to put on clean clothes. I was willing to bet the cost of my meal that Eli stank like the insides of my gym shorts. And yet, despite looking like a New York City hobo, he was still built like someone who could and would tear me from crotch to crown. His arms are the size of my thighs and his thighs are the size of my torso. His dusky skin hoarded shadows, making him appear even more dangerous. Which he was. Eli was a wrestling god at Rendview. And an honor student, and homecoming king, and staring at us.

"I could take him," I said, trying to look like I wasn't looking. "Anyway, he's mourning Cassie, not trying to get back with her."

Ben patted my hand. "Simon, I would love nothing more than to see you and Cassie sneak off to a quiet bedroom to fulfill your porniest fantasies so that you can finally move on with your life, but it's never going to happen. Ever. Not in your lifetime or mine. Not in a parallel universe where you and Cassie are the last human specimens on a planet ruled by poodles."

I leaned back in the booth and crossed my arms over my chest. "Your confidence in me is inspiring. No, really, I may weep. Here come the tears."

"Just keeping it real."

"Don't be mean," Coop said.

"Sorry," Ben said, but not to me. He and Coop got those silly looks on their faces that meant they were dangerously close to engaging in some full-frontal smoochery. Thankfully, a tall girl with long blond hair strolled over to our booth and saved me from that ungodly display. We waited for her to say something, but she stood there awkwardly for a long moment.

"Did you forget your lines?" Ben asked.

The girl shook her head. I noticed a long scar that ran along the bottom of her chin. "Ketchup," she said.

"It's not a vegetable, kids."

I kicked Ben under the table. "Don't mind Ben," I said. "He thinks he's funny when he's mostly just an ass." I grabbed the ketchup from the end of the table and passed it to her.

"You're Simon, right?" the girl asked. I nodded. "I'm Natalie Grayson." She smiled brazenly.

Something about that smile reminded me of—"Wait. We had sophomore geometry together, didn't we?"

"Yeah." Natalie's face lit up.

"What did the guy say when he got back from vacation and found his parrot's cage empty?"

"Polly gone," she said, and we both laughed.

Ben groaned and muttered something under his breath that sounded like "geeks," but I ignored him.

"Are you going to Cassie's party?" Natalie asked.

"Totally."

"What's the deal with the bartering thing?"

I'd already made Coop explain it to me a thousand times. I mean, I got the concept but didn't see the point. "You bring stuff to the party," I said. "And you trade it for other stuff."

"Like what?" Natalie stood holding that ketchup bottle with both hands. I was afraid she was going to squeeze a tomato geyser into the air.

Ben reached into his pocket and pulled out a little plastic bag with a dozen white pills in it. "Once people get shit-faced,

I'm going to make a mint with these. People will trade me anything for them."

"Drugs? Really?" Natalie did not sound impressed.

"They're baby aspirin." Ben put his finger to his lips and gave the girl one of his patented winks.

"I still don't get why," I said.

"For fun, dumbass. What'd you bring?" Coop asked Natalie.

She looked over at her table, which was packed with girls I knew by sight but not by name. They were the minor-league hitters. Not A- or B-list girls, but not part of the moo crew either. "I stole some tiny liquor bottles from my dad, and I have a guitar pick signed by Damian Crowley of Noodle Revolution."

Ben faked puking into my empty basket of fries. He hates NR. Hates. So much that he started an anti-fan club.

"You can totally trade up with that," Coop said, ignoring Ben's continued mock vomiting. "It's like that Canadian guy who started with a red paperclip and bartered his way up to a house. You could trade your guitar pick for a hot prom date if you played it right."

"Fat chance," Ben muttered, but we all ignored him.

Coop was giving me a look, this mental nudge that he seemed to think I understood. For the record, I did not. But, apparently, I wasn't the only person at the table who didn't get Coop, because Natalie was looking at him like he'd been speaking Parseltongue.

"Maybe I'll see you at the party, Simon," Natalie said, stuttering her way through the sentence, her earlier store of bravery seemingly all used up. "Thanks for the ketchup."

"Anytime," I said. "You need ketchup, I'm your man. Call me Mr. Ketchup. Or, you know, not."

I watched Natalie walk back to her table, where she said something to her friends that made them giggle and squeal.

An idea struck me. "Coop, you're a genius."

"Tell me more," Coop said.

"That thing you said about bartering a paperclip for a house. Was that true?"

"Indeed." Coop grinned at me, and then at Natalie. "You can do anything you want tonight, Simon."

"Then I'm going to barter for a kiss from Cassie. I'm going to tell her that I love her."

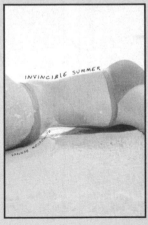

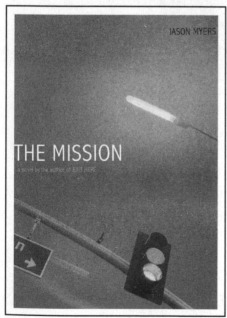